I0524586

A Chat with the Devil

and other short fiction

by George Arthur Lareau

SUFI GEORGE BOOKS
Tucson

A Chat with the Devil

Copyright ©2009 by George Arthur Lareau. All rights reserved under International and Pan-American Copyright Conventions. No part of this work may be reproduced or transmitted in any form by any means, electronic or mechanical, including photocopying and recording, or by an information storage or retrieval system, except as may be expressly permitted by the 1976 Copyright Act or in writing by the publisher.

ISBN 978-1885570-86-4

Sufi George Books: http://sgbooks.sufigeorge.net

A Chat with the Devil

Contents

A Chat with the Devil

A Chat with the Devil

In a rush to get home to fix supper and have it on the table on time, Marge zoomed through the parking lot, knowing it was a dangerous thing to do, but she was late.

Marge squealed into the driveway, got out and slammed her door, opened the rear door, picked up the two sacks of groceries, closed the door with her rear, and started a dash to the house.

She stumbled.

As she realized she was falling, she said a quick prayer. "Oh, Jesus help me!"

The groceries landed first, spilling across the lawn. She landed next, slamming her head against the edge of the sidewalk.

"Ooooh!" she said, rubbing her scalp, holding herself up on one elbow. Then she saw a red-legged hoof planted in the grass not more than four inches from her other hand.

Curiosity mixed with dread. She stared at it. She knew what it was, but actually seeing it took getting used to. She looked at it hard to see if it would go away; but it didn't.

"My goodness, Marge, such a tumble!" a soft voice soothed from above her.

A Chat with the Devil

She jerked her head up, like ripping off a Band-Aid, to get the sight of it over with. And there he was.

He was naked with red skin, but cloaked himself in huge soft wings. He stood with his arms folded across his chest.

He looked very handsome, not at all what she expected. In fact, except for being red and having wings and skinny legs with hooves, he looked rather normal.

This unexpected appearance made Marge uncertain.

"Are you the devil?" she asked hesitantly.

"In living color," he said, chuckling.

"Well, you don't have to make jokes about it!" Marge said. "I don't think it's the least bit funny! What are you doing here?"

"Just doing my thing," the devil said. "Just doing my thing."

"Well, don't just stand there, help me up," Marge said, then added, "no, forget that, I didn't mean that. I'll get myself up."

Marge got up and brushed her skirt off front and back. Then she put her hands on her hips and stared the devil straight in the face, quick little prayers for help racing through her mind.

"All right, devil. What do you want with me? You know I'm a good Christian. You can't touch me."

The devil reached out and touched her arm.

A Chat with the Devil

"Yes, I can," he said, laughing.

Marge jerked her arm away.

"You know what I mean!" she said.

"Okay, okay," the devil said, putting on a straight face. "I'm here to tempt you, to test your faith, you might say."

"Well, you won't get away with a thing," Marge said.

In her mind, she called on Jesus to help her and protect her.

Marge said, "Look, why don't you just give up and go away! I've got to get supper on the table."

"Look around you, Marge."

She looked around quickly and everything seemed normal. Then she noticed that a passing car was frozen in place, the driver looking intently ahead. The trees and bushes were perfectly still. There was a strange sound, rough but not very loud.

"What's that sound?" she asked.

"That's your grocery bag ripping," the devil said, pointing to the frozen bag not yet fully landed on the ground.

"Everything's frozen!" Marge said, accusingly.

"Yes, time is frozen. That's to give us time to talk. You see, supper won't be late after all!" he laughed. He gestured to the cement steps. "Why don't we sit over here and make ourselves comfortable?"

Uncertainly, Marge looked around again. Everything was still frozen.

A Chat with the Devil

"I can't just make you go away?" she asked.

"No, I'm afraid that this little chat is something you can't get out of, Marge. But, I'll try to be amusing so that you are not too bored, okay?"

Resigned, a little confused, Marge sat on the step next to the devil.

"Can anybody see us?" she asked.

"No, of course not. This is all happening in a split second, actually no time at all. Nobody will catch even a glimpse of us. Why, do I embarrass you?" he smiled.

"Something like that," Marge said. They were silent for a little while.

Then Marge said, "Well, go ahead and tempt me. Let's get this over with."

The devil laughed. "Ha! Ha! What shall I tempt you with? Something pretty? Something gold?" He laughed again.

Then Marge realized that she really was temptable. Maybe not with gold, but she had her weaknesses. She prayed for strength.

"I'm not going to sell my soul for gold," she said, as if the words were dirt.

"Then we are talking price," the devil laughed.

"No! I mean I'm not going to sell my soul for anything!"

"Suppose it's not your soul that I want?"

4

A Chat with the Devil

A shudder of fear swept through her. What could he want? she wondered anxiously.

"What if I wanted something much easier to give?"

"And what would that be?"

The devil looked at her sideways, smiling broadly.

"How about your attention?" he said.

"What would you want that for?"

"I have my reasons. What do you say, will you sell your attention?"

"I don't understand what you are saying. I mean, my attention, that's...what's that, that's just, like paying attention to something, is that what you mean?"

"That's it."

"You mean I wouldn't be able to pay attention to anything if I sold you my attention? No deal!"

"Of course I would let you keep it. You're right, you couldn't get along without it."

"Then, if I keep it and sell it to you, I don't understand."

"Marge," the devil laughed. "You are giving me your attention right this very minute. And I haven't even given you anything yet!"

"Well big deal, what am I supposed to be doing?"

"The point is, you are giving it to me and yet you still have it for yourself."

"Oh."

"I want more of it."

"So, now I get it! You want me to pay attention to you so I will stop paying attention to my Lord! No deal!"

"But you haven't heard what I'm willing to pay," the devil smiled. "You really should at least listen to what I can offer. Otherwise, you won't be able to say that you have been properly tempted, right?"

Trust in the Lord, trust in the Lord, she repeated to herself silently. She was afraid and she was curious. God forgive me for being curious, she prayed. God give me strength to endure, she prayed. Deliver me from this temptation, she prayed.

Then she turned to the devil and said, "Okay, devil. Let's hear it."

"Fine! Fine! That's the attitude! You know the old saying, opportunity doesn't knock twice!" he laughed.

He just smiled at her. She said, "Well?"

"Well. I'm thinking. I'm wondering what would really tempt you the most. How much I'm willing to pay. Of course, your attention is very precious to me, I'll admit that!"

Then Marge realized the trick.

"Wait a minute! I'm going to have to pay attention to what you say. Does that mean you're getting some of my attention for free??"

A Chat with the Devil

"Ah, you've found me out! Very well, I will pay you a little something in advance in exchange for the amount of attention you will give me to hear my offer. Does that sound better?"

"It sounds like I'm already making a deal with the devil!"

Marge said, but she didn't know how to get out of it.

"Okay, what's the deal? My God, I know I'm going to regret this."

"Please, dear!" the devil laughed, pretending to be upset. "You know I'm not supposed to hear words like 'God.'"

Marge didn't know if she was sorry. She could tell he was joking, and she studied him uncertainly.

"God, God, God, God, God!" Marge blurted out.

The devil laughed uproariously, stamping his hooves on the step and fluffing his wings.

"You're a funny lady!" he told her.

"How come that doesn't bother you?" Marge asked him, puzzled.

"Because we have the same God, silly!"

"But I thought...."

"I know. You thought that you could shake a cross at me and I would crawl into the nearest hole."

That's it! Marge said to herself. Why didn't I think of that before! She reached into her blouse and pulled out her cross pendant and held it toward him, trying to look menacing, but it was a very small cross and she felt a little foolish. The devil laughed at her again.

Disgustedly, Marge said, "Oh, boogers to you!"

"Now, let's be kind, let's not lose our manners," the devil chuckled.

"Dear God, please make the devil go away," Marge prayed aloud, staring the devil in the face.

"I'm not going away, Marge. Let's just make our deal, shall we?"

Oh yes, the deal, Marge thought, admitting a small amount of excitement. I wonder what I'll get for having to go through this, she thought.

"Okay. So tempt me."

"I think I know just what you'd like, Marge. I think you'd like it if your husband lightened up a bit with you. Am I right? Wouldn't it help if I took a little of that pressure off?"

"I never thought you'd come up with something like that!" Marge said, impressed.

"Oh, well. I'm a regular peacemaker these days. Things have changed so much, you know."

"I have to admit, that's not a bad deal. Considering you've got me stuck here anyway."

"Do you want me to pay you now?"

"You mean, right this minute? How could you do that?"

"Marge, it's simple when you know how. Besides, I'm in the business."

"Well, sure. But wait. Before you do it, tell me what you're going to do. I don't like surprises."

"Actually, I'm only going to demonstrate to you that I've already done it. I will reach back into time, to this morning, and arrange for your husband to experience an effective lesson in his office. He will learn about the equality of women and loosen his grip on his idea that women are born to be the slaves of men. He'll learn the lesson well, Marge. It will open his eyes up and it will stick. All you have to do is answer the phone and find out for yourself."

"Now, wait a minute. If time is frozen, then the phone call won't be real. You're not going to trick me!"

"You're not going to let me trick you, are you?" the devil laughed. "I have no intention of tricking you. I'll unfreeze time for the phone call. But first, you'd better get back down on the ground the way you were when I first saw you."

"Why?" Marge asked, not relishing the idea of getting on the ground.

"Because that's where you are right now. You'll feel an awful jerk if you have to snap over there from here!"

"Oh." She got on the ground, sprawled out, propped herself up on one elbow. She rubbed her scalp. "Ooooh, that smarts!"

A car passed, no one she knew.

"What a mess!" she said, looking at the litter of groceries. She began repacking them as well as she could, picked up the two sacks and hurried into the house. As she put the sacks on the kitchen counter, the phone rang.

Oh, I hope this won't take long, she thought, answering the phone.

"Honey? Have you started supper yet?"

It was her husband, and he sounded different, like maybe he was concerned about her.

"Oh, hello, dear. No, I just this minute got back from the grocery store. Why?"

"Listen, don't cook. Let me bring something home. What would you like?"

"What?? What have you done, Lewis? Did you spend our vacation money?"

Lewis laughed. "No, I didn't spend any money. I've been good all day! I just thought it would be nice for you to have a night off from cooking, that's all. Just showing a little appreciation, that's all. Okay?"

Marge still smelled a fish, but a night off from cooking, that was nice. It was a nice thought...if he really meant it, if he didn't have anything up his sleeve.

"Okay, but what's the occasion?"

"Listen, Marge, this is going to sound funny to you, but today I learned something and it changed my attitude about women, especially about you. That's the occasion. I'm just showing you that I care about you and that I want to treat you better than I've been doing. So what shall we eat?"

A prayer answered! Marge wasn't sure whether to trust it, but if this change in Lewis lasted, it would truly be a prayer answered. And maybe if it's a prayer answered, it would last. Fish and chips, she hated cooking fish and chips but loved eating them.

"How does fish and chips sound?"

"Great! See you in about an hour. I love you!"

Marge pulled the phone away from her ear and looked at it. He had never said that over the phone before.

Quietly, she said, "I love you, too."

She hung up the phone and looked out the kitchen window, staring wonderingly into space. It was too good to be true. Yet it seemed to be true! Thank you, Lord Jesus! she prayed.

Then Marge realized that she wasn't in a rush anymore! No supper to fix! What should she do? Something just for herself. She decided to sit on the front step and watch the world. She hadn't had time to just do nothing like that for ages.

She closed the door behind her and sat on the step.

The devil asked, "Satisfied?"

Startled witless, she spun her head to him. She stammered, "I, I forgot you were here, I, I didn't even remember anything about you!"

The devil laughed. "It had to be real, didn't it? I mean, you didn't want me to do anything phony, did you? You had to forget about me."

"Whew! You're something else, you know that? What am I saying! Praising the devil!"

"I accept the compliment!" the devil laughed.

"Oh, God," she moaned. "Let's get this over with!"

"You are satisfied, then."

"Yes! I'm satisfied!"

The devil rubbed his hands together with an exaggerated mock gleefulness. "Then I have you in my grip!" he laughed.

But it struck terror in Marge. Whimpering, she said, "What are you going to do to me?"

"Please forgive me, I didn't intend to frighten you. It was just my little joke, okay?"

"Well, what are you going to do to me?"

"Nothing painful, I assure you. I'm only going to entertain your attention. You'll have a good time, I promise."

"A promise from the devil. Now I've heard it all."

"I've held up my end so far, haven't I?" the devil said, pretending to look hurt.

Marge smiled. "Yes, you have done that. Okay, do it. Whatever it is."

A Chat with the Devil

It hasn't been bad so far, Marge thought. This devil hasn't weakened my faith any. Of course, it's unusual to have my prayer answered by the devil, but I did pray for it for a long time and I'm glad the prayer is finally answered. Even if it is by the devil. Is it okay to think that?

"Why did you have to pick a prayer?" she demanded.

"Because it needed to be answered. I told you, we have the same God. I didn't really do anything except pray your prayer for you. I can't help it if I'm better at praying than you are."

Marge smiled. Somehow, the devil's explanation made things all right.

Or am I falling into his grip? she wondered to herself. What if he's lying, deceiving me? Who ever heard of the devil saying prayers?

"I didn't know the devil said prayers," she commented.

"Just put me in the Amen corner!" the devil laughed.

"Do you have to joke about everything?"

"Everything!"

"Well don't make jokes about my religion."

"Certainly not. I was making a joke about prayer. I won't even discuss your religion."

This surprised Marge. "Why not? I thought that's what you were after!"

"I already told you what I'm after–your attention."

A Chat with the Devil

"But that doesn't make any sense!"

"You want me to make sense?"

"It's the least you could do. I'm not accustomed to talking with the devil, you know, and the least you could do is make sense."

"Okay. I have a bad reputation, you know. People say that I will take candy from a baby. And of course I do, but I'm trying to improve my image now and so I take the candy in such a way that the baby doesn't notice. The baby thinks it still has the candy. Understand?"

"No. What's that supposed to mean? I'm no baby."

"But you are. You have candy for me–your attention–and you have no idea what it is worth. If I told you what your attention is worth, you would demand the entire universe in payment. But I'm just going to steal it for free.

Marge started to say something but didn't know what to say.

"Of course, I will let you continue to have it. It's not worth anything at all to me unless I let you keep it."

"I don't get it. You want to steal something from me, yet you have to let me keep it or it isn't worth anything to you. I said to make sense!"

"Yes, ma'am," the devil said softly, hanging his head and peering at her sideways.

Marge couldn't help laughing.

The devil grinned. "Make sense. Coming right up!"

A Chat with the Devil

He became thoughtful and spread his hands on his bony knees. "Do you see that running boy frozen over there?"

Marge hadn't noticed him before. "Yes, I see him."

"How do you see him?"

"He's just right there."

"I mean, how does it work, this business of you seeing him?"

"I just look at him. Is that what you mean?"

"You just look at him? How?"

"With my eyes, silly! How do you think?"

The devil looked intently at her. "I think you look at him with your attention."

"Well what's the difference?"

"The difference is that the boy has been there all along, your eyes have looked that way several times, and yet your eyes did not see the boy. You did not see the boy until you paid attention to him. So where your eyes failed, your attention succeeded."

"So? I just didn't notice him before."

"You mean he didn't attract your attention?"

"I, he.... I didn't see him!"

"Until you paid attention."

"You're just playing with words."

"No, I'm playing with your attention. Your eyes cannot see unless your attention is in them. That's the difference, and that's what attention does."

"Why not just steal my eyes?"

"Because your eyes are useless without your attention."

"Bull."

"Why didn't you see the boy before I pointed him out?"

"I just wasn't paying attention! I mean, I just didn't look. I guess. Okay, I didn't pay attention. I see what you mean." Sarcastically, she added, "My hero!"

"Goodness! Is teacher's pet upset about learning a little something?"

"Well what's the point of learning something dumb like that?"

Pretending to be insulted, the devil said, "I thought I was showing you what I want to steal from you."

Marge relented. "Okay, so I see the difference I guess. But I don't see what the big deal is."

"Here's the difference. Is there a boy there?"

"Yes. He's right over there," Marge said, pointing.

"Was he there before you paid attention to him?"

"Of course he was. What a dumb question!"

"And is he there now?"

A Chat with the Devil

Marge looked again and the boy had vanished. "That's not fair! That's just a dumb trick!"

"A trick? Then how come you were able to see him just a minute ago?"

"Because you made him appear!"

"Then he wasn't there before you paid attention to him." The devil smirked.

"I didn't know you were going to make him vanish, you idiot!"

"Ooooh! Idiot! My, we're getting a little rambunctious, aren't we?"

"Oh, shut up!" All you did is play a dumb trick on me and now you're all smug about it. I suppose you're real proud of yourself."

"I am so ashamed of myself." The devil made a few tears appear in mock remorse.

Marge laughed. "Well, you should be."

She looked where the boy had been. "So what was the point of all that?"

"The point was to make you doubt. From now on, you'll never know if what you are seeing is really there or if it's just one of my tricks."

"That's rotten!"

"I am the devil."

"You're a rotten devil!"

A Chat with the Devil

"That's me."

"You're not even guilty about it! You...are...rotten!"

"Enough praise! Enough! You'll give me a swelled head!"

"Well, I'll fool you! I'll look at everything so carefully that I'll be able to tell your tricks! You won't get away with this!"

"Wonderful! That's just what I was hoping for!"

"Hoping for? Now what are you saying?"

"Why do you think I am making you doubt? I want you to examine reality carefully. I want you to be able to spot my tricks."

"But why?"

"Why, she wants to know. Because that is one way of stealing your attention!"

"That's not fair! You've already done it, and I didn't make any deal! You're supposed to be telling me ahead of time what you're planning, not just marching right ahead and doing it!"

"We only agreed on that for the one deal."

He's right, Marge thought. Darn! I'm already losing! No wonder, I haven't been praying!

Quickly, she prayed a fast but earnest prayer. Dear Jesus, don't leave me at the mercy of the devil. Please be here with me and help me. I'm not doing well without you. Please, dear Jesus, be here, and protect me!

A Chat with the Devil

"Since I've already stolen some of your attention, wouldn't you like me to pay you?"

It really is too late, she thought. The deed is done. That doubt is firmly planted. I know I will be paying much closer attention to reality from now on. No big deal, but still it should be worth something.

"Okay. What's my pay this time?"

"Let's think of something really grand. After all, I've stolen much more from you than you realize. Another prayer, perhaps?"

"Don't you go answering any more of my prayers! It's just not right."

"Then it will have to be something so wonderful that you haven't even thought to pray for it, something beyond your imagination."

Beyond my imagination! Marge thought. What would that be?

The devil sat, lost in thought. Then he stood up and paced on the sidewalk, slowly, thinking. He looked at Marge, shook his head and went back into thought.

"I have it!" he said suddenly, and sat down next to her again.

"What is it?" Marge asked, half-filled with expectancy, half-filled with fear.

"That's what it is!"

"What is it!"

"Knowing what is!"

"I've heard better than that at the check-out counter! What are you talking about?"

"How would you like to be able to know what is true? Be able to see something or listen to something, anything, any kind of experience, any kind of information, and know immediately whether it is true or not?"

"I already know what's true! Not about everything maybe, but I know all the important things. I don't need to know about everything. Who cares? This is a gyp deal. You'll have to think of something better than that."

"I don't think it's such a bad deal, Marge. Just think about it. You would be able to tell when a person is lying to you, just like that! And you would know when something is just made up or if it's real. You'd always know the right thing to do in any situation, just think!"

"Know the right thing to do? The right thing to do is what the Bible says. I know most all of that already."

"Well, I don't want to get into a Bible discussion with you. I'm really not interested in your religion."

"I still don't understand that. I mean, in church they're always saying how you want to destroy our religion and steal our souls."

"And I say different. You're hearing it from the source."

"So why should I believe you? You are the devil, you know."

A Chat with the Devil

The devil sighed. "Bad reputation, it follows you everywhere."

"Come on, you're really after my religion. Admit it."

"I admit no such thing. I don't even care for your religion. Why should I want it?"

"But you want to destroy it, don't you?"

"No! I don't care about it either way."

"Prove it."

"If you had the gift of knowing what is, you would know I am telling the truth. But do you want the gift? No. You'd rather have proof. Since when is proof better than actually knowing something?"

"How could I know? A gift like that from you wouldn't prove anything. You'd probably arrange it so that I thought every word you spoke was true."

"My, we are so suspicious! I am not talking about your thinking, I am talking about your knowing. There's a difference."

"Well, I don't see any difference."

"Of course not. You don't have the gift of knowing, not yet."

"I don't trust it. It sounds like a set-up."

"With the gift, you would know whether or not it's a set-up."

"Well, what if I didn't like the gift? Can I get rid of it?

A Chat with the Devil

Trade it in for something else, maybe?"

"The devil doesn't take trade-ins, I'm sorry."

"You pays your money, you takes your chances. Is that it?"

"I don't get any complaints. I turn a good deal."

"Probably nobody dares to complain."

"Nobody needs to complain. As I said, I turn a good deal."

"This gift of knowing doesn't sound like much of a deal. How would I know that I was really knowing the truth and not just some truth you put in me?"

"My dear, I'm crushed! I would never tamper with truth!"

"How do I know that?"

"If you had the gift of knowing..."

"I know," Marge interrupted. "Then I would know. But how would I know that my knowing was right?"

"Because knowing is right. There is only one kind of knowing, and it knows what is. Can't you understand? Rats, I always have trouble explaining this."

"Rats? That's how the devil swears? Rats?"

"Hey, I'm a nice guy!"

"That's not what I heard."

"If only you had the gift, you'd know what a nice guy I really am."

"That'll be the day."

"Okay, okay. I did have another idea, something else I could give you. But it's not as good a deal. You'd be losing out."

"I haven't heard a good deal yet."

"I was thinking that I could give you the gift of thinking. With this gift, no matter what you think about you can't make any mistakes. You always come up with the right conclusion. What do you think?"

"What do I think about thinking? Who needs it? I get my conclusions from my faith. You can't get that from thinking. Too much thinking can get you in trouble."

"Women! So hard to satisfy!"

"Well, then, offer me something useful!"

"Like what?"

"Maybe like money. Everybody can use money."

"That would be easy for me, but you'd have a problem explaining where it came from, wouldn't you?"

Marge thought about that one. "You're right, I'd have to lie about it."

"And that goes for anything else that's material. You'd have to lie. That's why I deal in nonmaterial gifts. Nobody asks where you got them. They think they just happened somehow. I can get away with a lot that way."

A Chat with the Devil

"Too bad I'm not short on nonmaterial things. Can't think of a thing I'm out of."

"How about happiness?"

"Well, sure, but you've already taken care of the major problem there, and besides it's not right to go around being happy all the time. That's just not the way life is. Life has to have suffering in it.

"Says who?"

"That's just the way it is because of sin."

"How about if I give you the gift of not sinning? No more sin, no matter how hard you try?"

"I should think you'd want me to sin. That's the devil's job, isn't it? Where did you go to school, anyway?"

"Very funny. Why should I want you to sin when sin causes pain and suffering? Do you think I'd have any business if I only offered pain and suffering? Who'd want to talk to me?"

"Well if pain and suffering isn't the work of the devil, who's responsible?"

"I really don't want to say this, but it's your religion. Isn't that clear to you? Isn't it your religion that makes you have pain and suffering?"

"Finally! You're attacking my religion."

"You made me do it."

A Chat with the Devil

"Ha! That's a good one! It's about time somebody made the devil do something."

"Let's not talk about your religion. We might never stop, and we have a deal to make here."

"How can the devil give the gift of not sinning?"

"It's quite easy, really. Are you interested?"

"It would be a great relief, to tell you the truth. But I wonder if it would get boring. I mean, the way things are now, I mean, I don't go out and decide to sin or like that, but if I do then I can be forgiven."

"It sounds like a little sin now and then adds some interest to your life, and you wouldn't want to lose that opportunity. Am I right?"

"You make it sound awful. I didn't mean it that way at all. I just meant that if I did sin–if–that I can be forgiven. So why do I need the gift of not sinning? If I can be forgiven anyway?"

"It's up to you. It's just an idea. Let me see what else I can think of."

"Would it mean that I couldn't even do little sins?"

"What's a little sin?"

"Oh, you know, things like having a cup of coffee sometimes, or maybe even a cigarette, or watching something on TV that I shouldn't."

"Absolutely, you wouldn't be able to sin at all, not even little sins."

"Then I don't want it. Keep thinking."

"But you could still do everything you wanted to, so long as you didn't hurt anybody."

"Everything? But what if some of the things I want to do are sins?"

"You mean you want to sin? Maybe I know a different gift after all!"

"No! You twist everything I say!"

"Then, what did you say?"

"I mean, nobody's perfect.

"Don't you want to be perfect?"

"Yes, of course. But, well, not yet anyway. I mean, I'm still young. There's plenty of time to become perfect."

"I see. You are one of those rare people who know that their life is going to go on and on forever."

"Not forever, silly! Nobody lives forever."

"Now there's an interesting gift, you know. Eternal life."

"You can't do that."

"Don't bet on it. You still don't know what school I went to, remember."

"You didn't really go to school."

"School of hard knocks."

A Chat with the Devil

"That I believe."

"So what do you think? Eternal life? I can do it."

"I don't trust you. You could just say it and then I'd have to wait years and years to find out if it's true."

"Which brings us back to the gift of knowing. If you had that, then you'd know you had eternal life. But you've already turned that one down."

"How could I know I had eternal life until I waited to see how long it lasted?"

"That's just how good knowing is. You'd know, flat out know."

"Sounds like bunk to me."

"There's only one gift left, and I don't think you've earned it yet."

"Only one? I thought you never ran out of tricks."

"These are not tricks! These are real gifts and there are only so many of them."

"Okay, so what's the last one?"

"I can make you God."

"Even if I believed you, I would not want to be God. Thanks anyway. Besides, the job is already taken."

"So? It's a big job."

"I am not looking for a job. Especially that one."

"I'm afraid, then, that I have nothing to give you. I have taken from you and I can't pay you for it. And I can't give back what I've taken. Are you sure you won't choose one of the gifts I've offered? Of course, if it's God, then I expect a little more from you."

"You're serious. That's it. A bunch of crazy ideas and you ask me to pick one."

"If you don't pick one, then you don't get paid. What can I tell you?"

"Maybe I could say an aunt died and left me the money."

The devil sighed. "Okay. How much?"

"Gee, I don't know. You mean I can have any amount I want?"

"Any amount you want. The bigger the amount, the bigger the lie."

"Oh, just forget it. I don't want anything at all. That's the deal."

"Okay, Marge. I won't argue. But if you change your mind, just make a wish. I'll get the message."

And the devil vanished. Marge sat on the cement step enjoying her break. The breeze was gentle and pleasant. It had been ages, it seemed, since she had been able to relax this way, have a little time to herself. She had an hour before Lewis came home. She felt like smoking a cigarette, but she didn't have any. Just as well, she thought.

A Chat with the Devil

She watched the boy running across the street. She noticed something strange about him, nothing she could exactly pin down. It was more as if the boy...wasn't real.

A Chat with the Devil

When I Was the King

We have a good life. We have enough skilled hunters that we eat well and enough skill among the women to keep us in furs. Because of my mind, which has many times helped others with clever solutions to problems, I have become the king. It is blazing to be the king. There are many hands of people in my kingdom.

According to our history, our people originated from a man and woman who descended from the sun. They were named Ahwa and Mettina. We are playfully irreverent and call them Maw and Paw.

We think very highly of the sun because it is our true source, the source behind Maw and Paw. Since we enjoy our lives, we are grateful to the sun.

I used to climb the mountain before I became king. I wanted to get closer to the sun, but it didn't help much. It's a shame, because it was one steep climb up there. Nobody else would do it.

And yet, looking back on it, there was a very great reward, a new idea. From the top of the mountain, I could see vast expanses of world, and it filled me with wonder.

Those of us who hunted generally headed toward our cave when the sun was highest in the sky, so we never suspected that there was all this world out there. I wondered, first, what it was all for. It was much too much world for my kingdom. I could not visualize that we would ever grow into so much space.

I wondered about this, waiting for the new idea. The new idea was there, as it always was, lurking just out of reach of my mind. I had to snatch it somehow, and the only way I could do that was to think it, but I didn't know what it was or what to think.

In all, I made three trips to the top of the mountain. Each time, the weather was clear and wonderful. From the top I could see other mountains, which amazed me. They were very far away, but there was no doubt that I was seeing mountains.

That seemed so important to me, yet I couldn't figure out why it should.

Then, I began wondering if one of those mountains might have a cave. And then an idea came–if it did have a cave, it might have a kingdom. More people!

I laughed it off. The idea that there could be more people seemed ridiculous. Then, I said, Well, why not? It's a powerful sun.

Eventually, I planned to send my best hunter, who was also my best runner, to the distant mountains to see if there were any people there. The problem was that I couldn't tell this to anyone or the people would laugh at the king.

I had to think of a more believable story. It would have to be a thunderstorm of a story, because on the strength of it a man was going to run for many, many suns.

A Chat with the Devil

I called my kingdom together around the fire one evening. I put on a very serious face and told them my story.

In my story, I had seen Maw and Paw from the top of the mountain. I had kept it a secret all of these suns. Maw and Paw lived in a cave in another mountain, very far away but visible from the top of our mountain. They were still alive!

My people became very excited. What did they say? one asked. I said, They were too far away to be heard. But they both waved to me. What were they wearing? another asked. It looked like bearskins, I said. Oooooh! they said.

My entire kingdom was soon at work preparing a pack of our finest gifts for my fastest runner to present to Maw and Paw, and preparing an elaborate costume for the runner to wear, including a necklace of mountain lion teeth.

In private conference, I told the runner, This mountain is very distant. It may be many suns before you can see it, but I have seen it three times and I promise you that it is really there. Your voyage is not ended until you reach those mountains and present our gifts to Maw and Paw.

Remember everything from your departure to your return and bring us the story of your adventures.

I also told him in a whisper, to make it seem very secret, There may be another kingdom there that also was started by Maw and Paw. If there is, give my crystal to the king, saying it is a gift of love.

My runner was named Tf. It didn't matter that it couldn't be said loudly because we were always fairly close together, we men.

A Chat with the Devil

With Tf going to explore the distant mountain for me, I felt like I was having an adventure myself, an adventure that, like my ideas, is unknown to me in specific terms for its duration, until I finally snatch its belly full of details. That would be when Tf returns.

Soon Tf was gone, and a great quiet spread throughout my kingdom. Everyone felt that a part of themselves was off to face the unknown, and they took it gravely. This was the first time anyone in my kingdom had ever left.

I knew that it would be perhaps the life of leaves before Tf returned; it was a long way, and a long worry for my kingdom. I was the only one who felt good. I had to do something for my people.

Already, no one said Maw and Paw any more. It was a respectful Ahwa and Mettina. I noted this, and made a plan to exploit it. I mean, why not–it was there waiting for me, and I couldn't think of anything better. I told them that I was going to share a secret. When Ahwa and Mettina left our mountain, they thought thoughts all the way to the distant mountain, leaving a trail for other thoughts to follow. By thinking certain thoughts, we can travel on that trail with our minds.

It sounded obscure to them, but I applied myself to teaching them what I was talking about, and they finally grasped the idea that thoughts are things that can be viewed as separate and distinct from the self.

And the more I explained it to them, the more I believed it myself. A trail of thoughts–perhaps I didn't just make it up, perhaps there really is such a thing. Maybe Tf has an actual trail he can follow. What a shame I didn't think of this before he left.

Of course, this only made sense if Ahwa and Mettina had never died. And I had to suppose that that was possible, since they came from the sun, and who knows what that would do for a life span.

Our legend was incomplete. So much of it had been forgotten, or never existed. Our legend didn't tell us what ever happened to Ahwa and Mettina.

They are not here, I reasoned, so if they are alive they must be somewhere else, and those distant mountains have got to be it.

My people were influencing me to take our ancestors more seriously. I had never given any deep thought to our legend. It was in the past, and I was interested in the future, where the new ideas are.

Now, though, this august couple was very likely to be an integral part of my adventure. This realization made my adventure really begin; I had some detail already. I wondered if my detail would agree at all with the detail Tf brought back.

At any rate, I devised a religion for my people so they could participate in Tf's quest. They had to begin by thinking thoughts in the direction of the distant mountains, close by at first, to see if they could catch the trail.

If they had a thought that seemed not to be their own, it would mean they had found the trail.

I gave my people the task of positioning their minds along various points on the trail, so that when Tf crossed the trail, which was likely, the closest person could swiftly fill Tf's mind with thoughts that a trail existed and how to use it.

No one was ever certain of success; it is not an easy thing to distinguish a visiting thought from one's own. But I give them all credit for working hard. They took advantage of every opportunity to sit in a quiet place and monitor their thoughts.

A day came when a woman was fairly convinced. She told her experience in detail to everyone in the kingdom (except Tf, of course) so that they could help her decide exactly what it was.

The spirits in the kingdom lifted immediately, not because any consensus was arrived at but because the possibility of success seemed close.

I figured I would wait until someone actually did it before I bothered with trying myself. Then I could quiz them and just do what they did. Why do the development work myself? I am the king, after all. My basic job is to keep my people's lives interesting and organized, and they gave themselves to me because I am the best of us that way.

Everyone in the kingdom belongs to me, you see; I own them. They all belong to my family, the kingdom. I have the right to abuse my privileges if I feel like it, but I always share my feelings openly, as we all do, and there can be no abuse that way. We understand each other so well that we see ourselves as a single, complex person.

Of course, I don't share all of my thinking. It would scare them half to death if I did. So I feel perfectly comfortable about couching my plans in terms they can accept and understand, even if I am not exactly telling the truth.

A Chat with the Devil

Tf was gone for a long time, as long as it takes a child to see many snows.

My people felt they were succeeding at their task, but were never completely certain about it. One day I decided it was time to check into it myself.

They had developed a simple technique. Face in the direction of the distant mountain (I had placed a stick on the ground pointing to it), and think of a stream of thought flowing in that direction. Other than that, their technique called for near thoughtlessness, stopping their own thoughts so that outside thoughts could be detected.

I did it, and it worked well enough to suit me. I found Tf already on the trail, aware that the trail existed and that it can be followed with thoughts. My first reaction was that this couldn't be right--Tf still following the trail! I thought he would be nearly home by now.

I skipped ahead of Tf to see what I could see. I rushed and rushed, but it still took a long time to find the end of the trail. It ended in a huge cloud of accumulated thoughts that filled a large area in and around a cave.

I felt buffeted around by so many thoughts and couldn't register anything clearly. It was chaotic. I warned Tf about this on the way back so he could think about how to prepare for it.

When I opened my eyes and stood up, I knew immediately that I was going to climb the mountain one more time. I told my people, packed my provisions, and was on my way the same day. I didn't know how they would manage without a king for a while, but my sense of urgency left me no choice.

Urgency or not, there is no fast way to climb the mountain. It is a true test of patience, and my life depended on remembering that. Patience is the virtue of the mountain, and to climb it safely one must exhibit the mountain's virtue.

I reached the top late the next sun, and could not see the distant horizon.

I felt I was too late, that I had missed whatever it was I was here for. I fell asleep full of disappointment. When the sun appeared, I immediately awakened and looked to the horizon. The distant mountain had grown into the sky. Soon, with better daylight, I saw that the mountain was on fire, and that what I thought was growth was actually billows of smoke. The mountain was on fire! Was it a signal? I wondered. What did it mean? Was it a response to me reaching the chaos with my thoughts? Can thoughts start a fire? It had to be a response. There was a contact from a distant kingdom—me. That was the first time there had ever been such a contact. It had to be a signal, a big enough signal for me to see.

Patience, I reminded myself, as I descended the mountain. I was eager to share this news with my people. Ahwa and Mettina have given us a signal.

They know we are here. They know we are here. But where will they live if they have burned up their mountain? someone asked. I hadn't thought of that. Let us tell Tf to invite them to join our kingdom, I was about to say, but then I wondered if I would still be king with them here.

Then I realized that if they wanted to come here, I couldn't stop them. So I went ahead and said it. Now, the kingdom felt great excitement. The prospect of seeing Ahwa and Mettina alive was an incredible possibility, yet that is just what may happen.

Secretly, I thrilled over the possibility that an entire kingdom may be joining us. Life would become so intensely interesting that I would be king forever, and never die.

I was tempted to travel the trail again, but I disliked my disorientation in that meadow of chaotic thoughts so much that I restrained myself. I could talk to Tf, but I didn't have anything to say to him, really. He was doing fine on his own, with the helpful thoughts from the kingdom.

Someone told me that Tf knew about the fire. He was close enough to see the burning mountain. It was, in fact, not very far away now, and he would reach it in just a few more suns.

Tf, of course, would not get caught in the chaos of accumulated thoughts because he had all of his resources with him, including the ability to admit a single thought at a time. Furthermore, his body would dominate his experience, gathering in all it can sense.

If there were people there, Tf would see them, meet them, and exchange information with them.

As it turned out, Tf didn't have a chance to visit with any leisure. One of my best people told me that Tf met a long line of people walking toward him, following the trail, on the very next sun after the sun of the mountain fire. He could not speak with these people because, strange as it seems, they spoke differently. However, they understood the words Ahwa and Mettina, which they pronounced Ahway and Mettinay. And they knew Maw and Paw!

By forgetting about trying to talk with these people, and instead concentrating on contacting them by way of the trail, Tf figured out that they were leaving the burned-out mountain, and were following the trail in search of a new kingdom. They had no idea if the trail led anywhere, but they had discovered its existence.

Tf invited them to join my kingdom, but could not adequately get across just how far away it was. Since they had met Tf just one sun's journey from the mountain, they could not understand that he had walked much farther than that.

Soon, there was a rush of communication between my people and these others from the distant mountain. The immediate disappointment of learning that Ahwa and Mettina were long ago dead, although they did indeed found the distant mountain kingdom, was quickly replaced by eagerness to contact these new people. Who had ever heard of such a thing?

Through Tf, they were already with them. There were many of them, enough to fill many caves. And the new people all thought that they would arrive at the new kingdom within a few suns, a conviction reinforced by the immediacy of thought contact on the trail.

My people had plenty of time to clean out many new caves, stock them with furs, and fill one cave with animal meat that had been dried in the sun, honey, apples and roots. In fact, they finished this work with enough time left to prepare the greatest celebration the kingdom would ever experience.

There was to be a big fire, with enough wood to last all night long. Two men made drums out of logs and animal skins, and practiced on them until, much to my relief, they made a pleasant sound. Several women practiced dances.

A sun finally shone when everyone knew that Tf and the new people were arriving soon. Everything was ready, but there was a lot of last minute sweeping of the grounds with branches and arranging of the wood pile. I think they just had to keep busy to contain their excitement.

I told my women to prepare me a costume that would make me look like king of the sun, so that the other king would be so awed by me that he would give himself to me. I wanted to resolve that issue right away.

It turned out they already had the idea, and were almost finished with a costume such as I had never imagined. It was woven strips of fur with a pattern of the sun on the breast. The headpiece was the head of a huge bear, to be adorned daily with fresh blossoms.

Tf ran into the camp one day before the sun was highest, his powerful muscles bulging as we had never seen before. A great cry went up, and the people crowded around him, asking him as many questions as they could manage as they steered him to where I was sitting.

I was overcome with joy at seeing Tf, and my tears flowed freely as I embraced him again and again. I gave him my seat and sat at his feet to honor him.

Our communications had been very accurate, and Tf actually had little new to tell us, except for one amazing thing that we had no way of learning from the thought trail. The new people had a strange and wonderful practice of sounding with their voices, so that they could imitate thunder, rushing water, birds, and many other sounds, which they produced all at once and in rhythms like a drum.

They were waiting their welcome a short distance away as Tf was telling us this news. Tf handed me my crystal, and a necklace of crystals, both gifts of the other king who did not want to be a king anymore. Tf said the other king felt that he was a failure because he had not been able to prevent his kingdom from burning. I was immediately relieved and filled with love and concern for this king.

We celebrated for many suns, learning all about each other, feeding each other, sharing furs with each other in the caves, and kept the fire burning for so long that the people got tired of throwing new wood into it.

All of the new people gave themselves to me, and I didn't even need to wear my new costume, which was too hot to wear anyway, although I couldn't bring myself to say this to the women who had made it.

My success as king was now so completely assured that I retired to my cave to think new thoughts. I was getting old enough to appreciate long periods of quiet and solitude.

Kill You

"I'LL KILL YOU!!" my father screamed. BUNG! His ring slammed across my head. I had no doubt that he would kill me. I ran. My younger brother caught up with me.

"You get bunged?" he asked in his seven-year-old voice, his eyes filled with tears for me.

Crying and rubbing my head, I was grateful for his sympathy. "Yes," I whimpered.

"What did you do?" my brother asked.

"Nothing," I said. "I moved the chair."

My brother cried for me. He got bunged as often as I did; he knew how it hurt. It hurt the head, that massive ring with the eagle with two heads on it with a diamond in the center. And it hurt the soul, because we never did anything wrong and it wasn't fair. We were too afraid of getting killed to do anything wrong, not when father was around anyway.

Father was the enemy. He was powerful. He was angry without notice, even in the middle of laughing. Killing could spring out at us, and did, at entirely unexpected moments. It made no difference who was around–he would just as soon kill company if they ever said anything, although we never saw this happen.

The enemy was too much for us. There was no way we could fight back or get even. There was no way we could get the enemy to stop. We got killed daily, and it was going to go on forever.

"I'm going to kill him," I told my brother.

"How?" he asked, believing me because I was two years older.

I tried to improvise a plan. "I'm going to throw that boulder at him," I said, pointing to a five-foot rock which was well-rooted in the ground.

My brother was skeptical. "You can't pick it up," he said.

"I'm going to take that Charles Atlas course and then I can pick it up," I said.

Now my brother believed me. We had both studied the Charles Atlas ad on the back of a comic book, and together had fantasized about being so strong that we could kill the enemy.

For some reason, we began attending Sunday School at the village Congregational Church. We were both delighted and mystified, at first, because we were never allowed to leave the house except for school. It must have been some profoundly rare influence of our mother, for father never had a good word to say about religion.

Soon, we knew about God and prayer. Immediately, we both got the same idea. We debated it at length, wondering if it was the right thing to do. We finally decided that I would try it out first, just in case it had consequences we didn't suspect. As the oldest, it was my sacred duty to face whatever risk was involved.

My brother listened, though, as we knelt together at the side of our bed and prayed.

"Please, God, make father die," I said softly. Nothing happened. It seemed safe. We listened to see if we could hear anything unusual downstairs, like something heavy falling to the floor. We heard father downstairs, talking.

I tried again. "Please, God, make father die. You don't have to do it right now, but please do it soon."

Several weeks passed during which we kept a close eye on father. He was as vigorous as ever. He killed us with the same regularity, usually with his fisted ring, but also with kicks and sticks. One time he chased me with a rake and broke it in two striking me over the shoulder. I think he was aiming for my head and missed. I ran as fast as I could, but he ran faster, screaming "I'LL KILL YOU!!" and stabbed me with the broken end of the handle, ripping my wrist open. My mother stood at the door screaming at him to stop, and finally he did.

I thought I was surely going to die from this killing. There was real blood this time. My brother hid behind a door, crying loudly, "Harold is going to die!" My mother was screaming at father. Everything was out of control and it seemed as if the world was upside down.

My brother and I decided that praying for father to die was too dangerous after all. Furthermore, it didn't work. After that, Sunday School was simply a chance to get away from father for a few hours.

It was clear that we would have to do it ourselves, since God was no help at all. Our most serious problem was attempting and failing, because we would get killed really bad in that case.

Our plots were endless and fantastic, but we didn't trust any of them enough. We would build great enthusiasm for a plot, try to convince each other that it would work, and then shift our attention to something else entirely.

One day, an uncle shot a bear in the mountain we lived on. It had been scaring people. We learned about guns that way. We thought about getting a gun, but we didn't know how to do it. We even speculated briefly on asking the uncle to shoot father, but quickly decided that would be imprudent. We thought about dressing father in a bearskin and telling him that there was a box of gold in the mountains.

Sometime later, another uncle died in a racing accident. We went to the funeral and saw him in his coffin. We both marveled at actual death. We had liked the uncle, but it was so interesting that he couldn't get up out of his coffin that we could think only about father being that way.

For weeks, we played at racing toy cars in the hopes that we could infect father with a fever for becoming a racer. We got killed often for making too much noise, but we endured it because it was a holy cause.

Although he never actually lost faith in my leadership, my brother decided one day to take the initiative. "I'm going to kill him myself," he decided one day, after a particularly severe bunging. I do not understand why I never felt the sympathy for my brother that he felt for me. Perhaps it is that I was a kind of protector for him, futile as it was, whereas he was a charge for me.

"I'm going to put a snake in his bed," my brother said through his tears.

"But what if it bites mother?" I countered.

"Oh," he said, stopping. "Well, then I'll put it in his car."

"But if they go shopping it could still bite mother," I said.

"Well, then I'll just get a log and bash him with it!"

"Don't worry, we'll get him killed," I said.

After school, I would often stop by the library and check out a volume of the Book of Knowledge. I had decided that if I became smarter than my father, then I would know how to kill him.

There was a section of fantasy tales in the Book of Knowledge, and my brother and I would spend long evenings reading the stories together. The stories were wonderful, not only because they put us into a much happier world but because they introduced us to marvelous powers that we could yearn for. Magicians offered possibilities that we could not ignore. We envisioned being able to disappear just as the bung was coming. What could father do then?

Invisibility was very inviting. Father wouldn't know where to strike. We could even taunt him, provided we were willing to remain invisible all the time.

Flying seemed an ideal solution, also, although we worried about forgetting how to do it at just the wrong time.

There was a lot of interesting knowledge in those books, but we found nothing directly useful for plotting a killing. Poisons were not described in any detail. The information about making iron and steel did not prepare us for making a gun. Although a powerful force, lightning was not something we could control. We did not have any friends for forming an army. Knowledge did not seem to be the weapon we were seeking.

Our despair at this additional disappointment malingered. Winter came and lasted for eternity.

We never admitted defeat. We merely stopped talking about it. Another year had passed and we had somehow survived it. We were now much older. For some reason, though, we decided to act much younger. We babbled endlessly in baby talk, and played more childishly than we knew was right for us. It was a kind of protection.

We both knew that we had but one solution. We had to endure long enough–many eons–to reach that magical day when we could walk away without looking back.

When There Was the Void

When there was only void, a time both past and future, a miracle occurred. Any occurrence would have sufficed; any occurrence would have been the first occurrence, and the first occurrence was the miracle because in the void there had never been an occurrence.

The occurrence was this: the void became aware of itself.

How this happened is unknown. Some say it was inevitable. Others say that because the void had no dimension the occurrence was therefore among the limitless possibilities. But these are speculations.

In fact, it was a small miracle. When the void became aware of itself, it was aware only that it was a void. But a rush of activity followed. Next, it became aware that it was aware. Then it became aware that it existed.

Then it became aware that it existed as awareness in addition to existing as void. This led to awareness of quantity, the numbers one and two—void, and awareness plus void.

Void was both void and filled. Void was void and void was aware and awareness was filled. Void was the prime, and though lifeless, reality and awareness were alive within it.

A Chat with the Devil

Awareness filled all of void and void remained itself.

And so came the number three—awareness, void, and awareness plus void.

Then came the awareness that it had in these numbers a language. With this language it remembered zero, which was its state before the miracle. With zero came the awareness of time relationship, before and now, and also awareness of memory. Then came awareness of possibility, after. Awareness used its language to think four, and four came to be the first abstraction, which is a future memory in time relations.

And then came wonder, for awareness wondered what four could be.

Because of language, awareness invented creativity. It had created four. With creativity, awareness created something to be four. It could not create void because void was its parent. It could create more language, but five was as meaningless an abstraction as four. It could not create more memory, for there was nothing more to remember. It could not create new relationships because there were already the only possible three.

Therefore, awareness divided itself into two entities. For itself it retained memory, and it named itself One. In the other it placed language, and named it Four. One discovered that it remembered the language. Four discovered that it could reconstruct memory. Thus, One and Four were substantially equals.

Four recreated complete memory so that it understood that it was in the void. And it remembered One. Four communicated with One, in this way: We are both in the void and I am from you. One responded: We are both in the void, and you are myself.

Four then grasped creativity and divided itself. Four introduced Five, which meant: Out of the void has come another of our equals, and our language has increased.

Then Five announced: Out of the void and into the company of equals. Equals, I have a new creation to propose.

One and Four attended while Five explained: Let us differentiate ourselves and combine into one. One shall remember zero, Four shall think of six, and I shall take positions near you, first on one side of One, then between you, then on the other side of Four, and we shall combine into complex patterns.

One and four were motionless while Five darted about, first calling out 5-1-4, then 1-5-4, then 1-4-5. In this way, the three of them created complex additions to the language and became aware that the language could be extended infinitely.

One declared: I understand it. 5-1-4 means more-first-next.

Four declared: I understand it. 1-5-4 means was-is-was.

In this manner, One, Four and Five continued to divide and build their language until they were able to form very complicated thoughts. After some time, they became a large community adept in handling the thoughts, and their eloquence multiplied greatly.

As their thoughts multiplied, they gradually discovered something of tremendous importance. It began with playfulness, since the void did nothing to inhibit their activities. They played with certain thoughts especially because of their pleasant harmony, and gradually these thoughts assumed an existence independent of their memories or awareness. They discovered they could create thoughts that had existence of their own. It wasn't long before they discovered the challenge of manipulating such thoughts into concepts.

Concepts, they soon realized, had enduring substance because they were composed of a network of independent thoughts that fortified each other, and the concept had a greater reality than the sum of its thoughts. This was startling to them, but soon they began assembling concepts into combinations that created an even greater reality.

This was very exciting to them, and in their enthusiasm they had difficulty remembering that these super-concepts were resident in their awarenesses which in turn resided in the void.

Their language flourished, and they steadily created new challenges for themselves, meeting them and then thinking up some more. They developed imaginations and utilized them endlessly, until they had created such a profusion of super-concept realities that the void was filled with a chaos of possibilities.

As the oldest, One was the first to pause and observe what had happened.

One called the multitudes together for a conference. It took some time for everyone to stop what they were doing and attend to One, but finally they were all gathered and for the moment all creation stopped.

A Chat with the Devil

One delivered the following: We have become highly skilled, but look at what a mess we have created. We have filled the void with a total confusion of realities that relate to each other only in the most chaotic fashion. Now that we have our skills, let us cooperate in the creation of one grand super-concept.

The idea was timely, and everyone wanted to know what it would be. One had no idea. Four, however, had a suggestion.

Four suggested: Let us clear out this mess and then fill the void with an orderly arrangement of super-concepts that are so well integrated they equal an entirely new kind of reality. Then, let us devise a way in which we, ourselves, can live in and explore that new reality.

A great cheer went up, although the idea was still vague. However, they agreed to develop the super-concept by working in harmony.

Thirty-million-four-thousand-eighteen suggested a name for the project: Let us call it The Universe!

The plan developed rapidly. The void would be filled with lights, spaced distantly so that the nature of the void would be preserved. Each light would be assigned to a group who would be responsible not only for keeping the concept adequately in awareness so that it shone continuously, but also for decorating the light with a ring of colorful balls.

The most proficient groups would decorate one or more of the balls with a pattern of changing concepts that emerged into reality and then were replaced by new concepts. Among these decorations would be concepts that were suitable for short-term occupancy by awarenesses, and which would provide the intoxication of being lost in their own creations, with no awareness of their true natures, and with the challenge of exercising their creative impulses within severe limitations.

After much experimental thought, the concept of man developed, and he was created with layer upon layer of concepts until just the right vehicle was accomplished.

Great leeway was allowed for this creation, since the whole idea was to face challenges with only residual creative power available, a welcome diversion from their natural state of unlimited creative ability.

Thus, awarenesses began populating their own concepts, becoming lost in them for short spans of time, so constrained in the man-body that only slowly were they able to rediscover their ancient idea of working in cooperation.

Thus it happened that a single and tiny miracle made The Universe possible, and provided awareness with creative challenges that continue to expand.

A Chat with the Devil

Perfume Shop

I am walking in Old Delhi, a rich American which is news to me. They are surprised here—they dash up to me from all directions to speak with the American—that I prefer their simple white pajama outfits to American clothing. To them, I am dressed far below my station. They sense some mystery when they ask me, "You like this clothes?" I assure them, and they pass it off as one of my enviable privileges.

I don't know the name of this street. It is very crowded, from sidewalk to sidewalk. There are very few automobiles, which provides stage for the seemingly hundreds of means of conveyance.

Many walk, some with the help of sticks. There are bicycles, motor scooters, human-pulled rickshaws, ox-drawn bicycles, wagons, and a camel. We are all squashed together, working at getting past each other. There is a bull on the sidewalk, coming toward me, its horns almost brushing people.

Most of the stores are no larger than a restaurant booth. The owner must get in first and then set up his counter and wares.

They are all hawking, the street is alive with a hundred melodies floating through the clamor. Here is a man in my way who seems to be dying. He is in front of a street barber who is hawking for customers. No one considers him, and so neither do I. I am thinking that I should buy some kind of souvenir.

I am passing many small shops, and here is a wrinkled old man behind a board selling perfumes. He has three pint-sized bottles of colored liquid on the board, and several half-ounce bottles. I have this hippie prejudice against perfume because it isn't natural, but the colors are pretty and it's only a souvenir after all. I squat down and pass the colors by my nose. I choose one at random. He pours from the large bottle into the tiny one, very carefully, so carefully that I become a little tense. I pay one rupee and walk away.

I am smiling and feeling good, because I will bring a little piece of India home with me.

Pookie Gets Spooky

Sarah put her doll in its chair at the little table, and admonished her.

"Now you sit right there, Pookie! And don't make a mess of the table! You sit still while I get the tea."

Sarah swung her long braid behind her and walked to the kitchen, her head thrown back haughtily, striding in long steps, her arms swinging broadly.

The tea kettle was whistling. She reached for the teapot in the cupboard and filled it with hot water. Then she opened another cupboard and brought out a canister of tea and placed it on the counter.

She watched the clock for exactly one minute, emptied the teapot, measured in the tea and filled it with the tea kettle. As she put the tea kettle back on the stove, her finger touched the hot kettle. Drawing her stung finger back quickly to her mouth, she whimpered, "Mommy."

But Mommy was working at the church. Sarah was babysitting Pookie.

Carrying the teapot carefully with her left hand as she sucked on her finger, she made her way back to Pookie with slow, cautious steps.

Pouring Pookie's tea, she said, "There, Pookie! That's for being a good girl while I was gone!" She poured her own and took a seat.

Pookie said, "I'm always a good girl."

Sarah smiled. She thought she had imagined Pookie's voice, as she had been doing since she was a little girl. But the voice was echoing softly in the room. It was not in her head!

She looked at Pookie carefully. Pookie's bright red pigtails hung limply. The checkered shirt and overalls looked like they always had. But the huge painted eyes were shiny!

She couldn't take her eyes off of them. They glistened, as if they had a fresh coat of nail polish.

Sarah gave the living room a quick once-over to see if there was some new source of light, perhaps a reflection from a car windshield, but she saw nothing unusual.

She looked at Pookie again, and saw that the teeth were glistening, teeth that had not been repainted in years!

She leaned over close, and in a tiny, quavering voice, Sarah asked, "Pookie?"

In an instant, Pookie's face burst into living flesh.

Sarah reacted twice. First, she flooded with joy. Her Pookie was alive! Second, she recoiled in horror. She was crazy!

As if she could read Sarah's thoughts, Pookie said, "Don't worry, you're not crazy."

A Chat with the Devil

Pookie spoke! But no, I'm crazy! Sarah thought.

"Please say something to me, Sarah," Pookie said. "I can talk, we should talk."

"You're not real. I'm hallucinating this."

"So I can prove to you that you're not, Sarah."

"Ho...how can you prove it? You're it."

"And everything else isn't it, you should notice."

Sarah stared for a moment, trying to figure out what Pookie meant. Of course! What else am I hallucinating?

She looked around the room. Everything was completely normal.

"If you are hallucinating, so how come it's just me, I'd like to know?"

If I'm crazy, then I should be hallucinating about lots of things!

"I see the lamp isn't so soft yet that it's melting," Pookie said snidely.

"How did you get to be such a smart mouth?" Sarah demanded.

"So now you're going to hit me, I suppose? It's not enough for a doll to have a mouth, it has to be particular?"

"I'm sorry, Pookie. This is just really strange."

"So if it's not that you're so crazy, then what is it, I suppose you want to know?"

"How come you can follow my thinking?"

"Very good, Sarah. That's the first part."

"What first part?"

"The first part of the answer. What this is, remember?"

"Well, I missed it. What is the first part?"

"I can follow your thinking. Maybe I can do this because I'm a million miles away, maybe not."

"You mean...you mean that you are in my thoughts?"

"No, I just follow your thoughts on television. Of course I'm in your thoughts, where should I be, I wonder?"

"Then, doesn't that mean I'm crazy?" Sarah panicked.

"To have such thoughts? A crazy thought, that's what I am to you. After all these years I am treated this way," Pookie pouted. "Just see what I have come to!"

Sarah stared hard at Pookie, trying to see through her, trying to make her go away.

"Sarah, dear, your tea is getting cold. Why not sit down? We can talk until you figure this out. Take a little tea with Pookie."

Well, that makes sense. I may as well talk with Pookie until I figure this out. There's no big rush, Mommy won't be

A Chat with the Devil

back for hours.

As if uncertain of her welcome, Sarah edged into her chair, carefully eyeing Pookie.

Pookie smiled and nodded, saying, "That's a good girl. Now. All these years together and never a chance to talk. Such a shame, don't you think?"

Feeling foolish about actually talking with her doll, Sarah answered, "Yes. I guess I did all of the talking for both of us."

"So tell me. I've been dying to know. How did I get the name Pookie?"

"Oh, I remember. When I first got you, we played peek-a-boo. It came from that," Sarah said. "You were so big then!"

"This I like to hear, I suppose? As you grow bigger, I grow smaller?"

Sarah laughed. "I'm sorry! But you didn't really grow smaller."

"What's 'really,' I'd like to know? A minute ago I used to be big?"

"I was remembering how you were bigger than me. You were so huge then!"

"Now I'm huge again, let me keep up."

"Well, come on! Don't be so silly! It's all in how you are looking at it! When I was little, you seemed big to me. And now I'm big!"

"So I haven't grown a bit," Pookie pouted.

"No, I'm sorry, Pookie. You haven't changed at all."

"I'm talking and she says I haven't changed."

"Well, except for that, I mean, you've certainly changed today!"

"So maybe you are wondering again how come I'm talking?"

Sarah sighed. "I suppose. I've got to get this figured out before Mommy comes home."

"It's all so simple, a minute or two and we'll be done."

"Then let's hear it."

"You already know I'm in your thoughts."

"None of my other thoughts talk."

"None of your other thoughts get talked to as much as much as me."

"So what does that mean?"

"I'm supposed to listen for years and not become real in your mind?"

"Then it's okay?"

"Okay? It's all right, I don't know if it's okay, but it's all right."

"What?"

"Suppose you tell me, Sarah, is it okay? For me, it's all right."

"You mean, is it okay with me? Do I mind?"

"Sip your tea, dear. Think it over."

"It's up to me? If it's okay with me, then it's okay?"

"Okay with you, okay with me," Pookie said. "Sip your tea."

"Mommy doesn't have to know?"

"You can explain this to your Mommy?"

"Will she be able to hear you?"

"Now she can hear your thoughts?"

Sarah sipped her tea. It was all too absurd. And too real.

"What am I thinking right now?" Sarah demanded, forcing an image of her Mommy into her mind.

"You burned your finger. You want your Mommy."

The rest of the image flooded into her mind. Yes, she thought, I was thinking of Mommy being right next to me when I burned my finger!

"How about now?" she said, thinking of the lamp that wasn't melting.

"No lamps melting today," Pookie said.

"And now?" She thought of the tea kettle.

"Hot tea kettle."

"I guess you really can read my mind."

"This you didn't already know."

"I suppose I did. But I had to make sure." Sarah added, "Your face looks so real."

"You can thank yourself for that," Pookie said.

"I just made a decision. You're okay with me. You'll be my secret."

"So let's talk."

Suddenly excited, Sarah said, "Okay! Tell me something. You're the know-it-all!"

"So you know it all? Twelve years old and this is it?"

"Not me! Oh, well, I mean, I see what you mean. If you are in my thoughts, then you know what I know. But you know more than that! You knew how to explain this and I didn't."

"You knew. So many things in the way at first."

Sarah thought. She said, "I see."

Reality 101

A hand shot up; it was that pesky Arnold who always interrupted everything I said.

"Arnold, what is it now?" I sighed.

"Mr. Johnson, if reality is like a dream, how come I can't see it with my eyes closed?"

Kids these days! I used to wonder if education would really be that much different in the year 2000. The answer is in, that's for sure. I'm teaching reality theory to first graders, and they understand it better than I do myself.

"Arnold. What I said was that reality is made of the same stuff as dreams. I wasn't talking about how we see it, just what it's made of. Okay?"

It seemed to make sense to Arnold. He nodded and squinched up his face in thought. For two summers I had taken the continuing ed courses in the new reality. I had been "selected" as one of a new breed of teacher. I had learned what to say. And it was all preposterous, I don't care what the Department of Education says.

Arnold again! "Mr. Johnson, last night I dreamed that I was flying higher than the trees."

"That's good, Arnold. You'll be learning about dreams in second grade, okay?"

All I really had to do was deliver the material in the DOE outline, if these kids would just let me stay on track.

"Reality is all made of the same thing. This is true of ordinary reality and it is true of the reality in dreams. Reality is inside of our minds. Yes, Arnold."

"Mr. Johnson, can you see my mind?"

"No, Arnold, I can't."

"My daddy says that reality theory is against the Bible."

"Your daddy is not in danger of flunking first grade, Arnold. As I was saying, reality is in our minds. When we think something is real, it is because we think it is real, not because it is real. Arnold...."

"Mr. Johnson, when I was flying in my dream, I thought it was real. I tried to fly to school today and it didn't work. I scraped my shoes."

Enough is enough. I'm supposed to deal with a statement like "I scraped my shoes." From a first-grader. Right. Well...I really am supposed to deal with it.

"Arnold, you really did fly in your dream, because you thought you did. If you want to fly to school, then you must think you are doing it."

A Chat with the Devil

Give me a break. I'm really teaching this claptrap? This is the kind of new generation I'm helping to create? This is going to save the world?

Arnold is smiling a little too much. And he's not looking at anything in particular. Now, he's floating above his desk, and now is swooshing around the room in wide circles, pedaling his feet as if he's on an imaginary bicycle, balancing with his arms outstretched.

"Arnold, get back to your seat immediately!" Did I say that? I'm flipping out, right? Now three more of them are flying, playing follow the leader behind Arnold.

"In your seats, all of you!" I shout. No good. Half the class is flying now. Should I just ignore them? This isn't real! It's all in my mind! I'd better stop shouting at them! They must all be in their seats, thinking I'm crazy!

Too late. My shouting has brought the principal, Mrs. Alford. She's standing in the doorway, mouth hanging open, staring at the formation of flying first-graders.

"What have you done, Mr. Johnson??"

What have I done? Quick, I have to say something!

"Mrs. Alford, it's that damned Arnold's fault! He started the whole thing! He refuses to understand a word I say!"

A Chat with the Devil

Sheila and Harry the B

When she puts the vegetables on to sautee, Sheila knows she has about 30 seconds and she studies Harry through the crack in the door, counting slowly to herself.

Harry is celebrated as everybody's favorite bartender. Sheila hears his high laugh come over the crowd. Harry is joking with the customers again, and tasting a wine someone has brought him.

"That man," she mumbles to herself, giving Harry another good look, "I don't know how I'm going to do it, but that man is too good to be anybody else's but mine."

A waitress comes into the kitchen and snatches a plate off the shelf with a careless whisk. Sheila is pained and shouts, "You be careful with that, now!"

Ahmed the busboy walks in and she tells him, "Look at that! They show no appreciation for fine cooking! Treat it like slop!"

Ahmed doesn't speak English so he smiles and says a strange thing.

A Chat with the Devil

"Oh, I've cooked these meals so many times I do them perfect, just out of habit," she tells him. "Can you blame me for being upset when they don't show any respect for a well cooked meal?"

A mouthful of syllables spills from the boy, and he leaves.

"Oh, what do you know?" Sheila shouts after him.

It's quiet for a minute and Sheila drifts back to it. She says to herself, "I wasn't bad looking once upon a time. And if I have to get looks to get Harry, then I'd better get to work on it." She puts a half eaten buttered, fresh baked biscuit down on her cutting block.

"Oh, I'm feeling old!" Sheila sighs, and whips her oily blonde hair behind her. "Ten years behind a stove and where am I? Behind a stove. It's certainly about time I snap out of my stupor."

Now it's winter, though it's always summer in the kitchen. Sheila is much slimmer, and her hair is clean. She has a little ways to go, but she's looking good. Harry the B, he's famous as a bartender and is becoming famous as a gourmet as well.

"I'm going to start fixing him gourmet meals!" Sheila blurts to herself.

It is the dawning of a second phase in her campaign to catch Harry the B, for little seems to have come of the first. She has Harry the B's eye, but she doesn't yet have his true interest.

Her hand is ready to snap her fingers. She takes one more look through the crack in the door and her fingers snap by themselves. Without pausing to heave a breath, she plans her attack on the public library for books that will help her win over the gourmet palate of Harry the B.

Months pass. Sheila gets up from her chair by the window, puts down her library book and stretches. Her coffee table is littered with cooking books and her apartment is a permanent mess.

"Well damn!" she says, looking at the clock. "I'd better get at least some sleep tonight!"

"That man!" she says to herself, "putting myself through all of this just so I can get that man. He had better be worth it." A yawn later she is asleep, and she dreams of preparing gourmet meals which are raved about in the newspapers.

One day, a man comes into the kitchen and says, "Are you the cook?"

"Yes," Sheila nods, too busy to look up.

"I'm with the paper, and Harry the B gave me a little taste of that Hollandaise sauce, you know, he says, Here, see what you think of this! and it's not quite Hollandaise, though, is it? I wonder if you'd tell me how you make it? For the newspaper, of course."

Sheila thinks about the sauce, about the past year and the ton of books, about the long hours she spent just learning to taste, about how she has turned her trade into an art. With excitement not showing, she thinks about having her recipe published. She says, "What do you mean, newspaper?"

The man says, "Like the articles about Harry the B, Best Bartender in Boston. I wrote most of those. Harry the B, he owes it all to me. Of course, I'm primarily the culinary arts editor."

The reporter waves away and says, "Well forget that right now. I'm thinking of something like, Harry the B Best-Fed in Town! Secret Recipe Revealed! Get a few pictures of you, of course."

"Well, some luck is better than no luck at all," Sheila says.

One day the owner comes in and says, "Sheila, when you've got a minute."

"I got a minute right now," Sheila says.

"Well, these special meals you've been cooking up for Harry, they've created quite a sensation you know, and I was thinking if we could put some of them on the menu, because God knows we've got people asking for them, and we can ask a good price, too, and I can give you a nice raise, too, and anyway what do you say?"

Sheila says, "If you want to give me a raise, you clean up this kitchen!"

"Two veal Harry the Beees," a waitress calls, her voice echoing off sparkling clean walls and fixtures.

Ramon, the storeroom man, strides into the kitchen, morning edition waving in his hand, beaming at Sheila. In a thick accent he says, "Look! This is you! Look what it say. Best chef in Boston! Chef, that mean cook! Oh, I am so happy for you!"

Sheila nearly cries because although she's been getting calls, mostly very wonderful calls, it is Ramon and his outstretched arms that make it feel real to her. She feels an immense wave of relief, like she has her arm around the horn of the mountain at last.

Harry the B bursts into the kitchen, newspaper in hand, and says, "Sheila! Look at us! The best bartender in Boston next to the best chef in Boston!"

He laughs, "And I'll bet the best-looking couple in Boston, too!" and hugs her and kisses her enthusiastically on the cheek.

Sheila has a feeling like energy is coming out of the floor and sweeping into her through her feet. She comes into herself all of a sudden. "I actually am this new person everyone is talking about!" she says to herself.

Sheila pulls away suddenly and says, "You want to know something, Harry the B?"

Harry looks at her and sees she has this crinkle-eye look.

Sheila tosses her locks and says, "This is Sheila the C you're messing with now!"

A Chat with the Devil

The Fly on My Knee

The fly on my knee was thinking, "I made this knob get big."

I couldn't understand it. The knob was apparently my knee. But it hadn't changed size. To me, that is.

Then I saw. To the fly, my knee had become larger in the sense that it now filled more of its field of view than when it had been across the room.

I stayed tuned in to the fly, brushed it away, and suddenly saw the room twisting, gyrating, crazily. Everything was changing sizes, like they were being puffed up with air, only to suddenly exhale. And the speed of it all was dizzying.

I sent to the fly, "Things certainly look different from your point of view."

"Whatever do you mean?" the fly asked.

"In my reality, things do not change size. And they stay put, usually. In yours, they huff and puff."

"Huff and puff, is it?" the fly retorted. "I suppose you don't see that I make my reality get bigger and smaller. Hmpf!

Give credit where credit is due!"

"What about closer and farther away? Do you make your reality do that, too?"

"Such strange ideas! You must be one of those dimensional monks I've heard about. Are you?"

"No, I'm not. At least, I don't think so. What is a dimensional monk?"

"It is obvious that you were not raised around here," the fly said. "A dimensional monk is a radical and insane denizen of the mountains who teaches foolery about a dimension called space."

"So you do not have that idea, about space?"

"I most certainly do not. I can believe my own eyes, can't I? I have enough of them. And it is perfectly obvious to me and to everyone else that reality exists in front of our eyes, like a screen. Space? Moving ourselves around? It'll never catch on."

"It looks very different from my part of reality. In my reality, I can see you flying through space. You even landed on my knee."

"Flying? That's one of those ridiculous notions that goes along with space. 'If there's space, then we can fly through it.' Insanity."

"Not insanity, just something different."

"Well, I don't need anything different. I find it quite satisfactory to be able to make anything I please grow right up to my face or shrink away into the little-bitties. I can make anything vanish completely just like that. I suppose you space people can do that?"

"As a matter of fact, we can't," I said. "But we can move, from one real place that stays just as it is while we're gone, more or less, to another place that stays just as it is while we're gone, more or less, that will be more or less as we expected it to be. Your reality is always changing. Ours stays still much, much longer than yours."

"I'll have you know that I can summon up any image that I've had previously, as long as it wasn't too long ago, more or less. That sounds like what you are talking about."

"For example, you landed on my knee three times before I took you seriously."

"Landed! You space people! I simply recalled the image, and bloom, there it was."

"Listen. You must feel your wings buzzing when you fly."

"Buzzing? That's the adjustments, the sound the adjustments make, that's all.

"Does it interest you that I can see you fly in my reality?"

"You have only two eyes and no evidence. Why should I take you seriously?"

"Why, why," I stalled, trying to think of an answer, "well, I suppose because I am a witness to it. Do you believe in witnesses?"

"Only when they confirm my own observations. Otherwise, how can I relate to them?" the fly said.

"Then I suggest that you tune in to my view of reality, just as I am now tuned in to yours."

"What kind of image is that? I'm not really expert, you know, on summoning up images deliberately. I confess that most of my images are spontaneous events."

"It's not an image at all. It's not your usual way of seeing things. It's my way, a new way to you. I guess you really don't know anything about it, do you?"

"Oh, I've listened to the monks some, just to hear what they were saying, of course, nothing more. I've heard these space ideas."

"Then that's a start. Make an assumption, for the moment, that there is something to this idea of space, that you might actually experience it yourself. Can you do that much?"

"It is a completely unreasonable act, but I will go along with you. This is, after all, my first contact with an alien, I suppose that's what this is, after all, my first contact with an alien, I suppose that's what this is."

"Now, imagine that you have wings on your back, and that when you feel the buzzing it means you are flying. When you fly closer to things, they seem to get bigger, but actually they haven't changed size at all. Can you imagine that?"

"A warped view, that's what it is! Pure imagination and poppycock. Okay, I will attempt this," the fly said.

A Chat with the Devil

I tuned out and saw the fly on my knee. Quickly, I tuned back in to see if the fly was seeing space. And it was!

"So, Miss know-it-all, what do you think of space now?" I taunted.

"It's all my imagination and you know it. But I admit that it is a fascinating experience, quite convincing, really. Even though it's only imagination, I thank you for bringing it my way....space alien."

A Chat with the Devil

Under Bad Fred's Bed

Things could be worse, Connie says to Bad Fred, and she wipes down the bar and Bad Fred drinks down his bottle since he has to pick it up for Connie's bar rag anyway.

Don't fucking tell me about worse, Bad Fred says. Things are worse; I don't need you telling me about fucking worse. Bad Fred says, I go to McDonald's for breakfast this morning and the bitch is fucking sleeping and she gives me my bag with no fork and no knife and no fucking jelly and no fucking salt and pepper and I pick up the bag high and dump it out on the counter and I tell the bitch, There's a lot of fucking shit supposed to be in this bag, and it fucking ain't in the fucking bag, like I'm supposed to eat this shit with my fucking fingers? And there's scrambled fucking eggs all over the counter and I say, Fuck your breakfast, just fucking give me my money back, and I throw the empty bag at her.

Do you get your money back? Connie says.

Fuck no, I hock a louie on the bitch and leave. Gimme another beer.

Hock a louie? Connie says, reaching into the cooler.

A Chat with the Devil

Flip a clam, Bad Fred says but Connie still doesn't get it so he says, I fucking spit a gob of snot pudding on her.

Gross, Connie says.

Lands right on her ugly puss.

Well that makes it easy to wipe off, not like it gets on her uniform, Connie says.

Fuck you, Bad Fred says. How come you always got to have this cheery fucking attitude about every fucking thing? Jesus fucking Christ.

Hey fuck you, Connie smiles. Like I said, things could be worse. What's wrong with that?

Like I'm so sure you know all about worse, Bad Fred says.

Like I'm so sure you know anything about me at all, Connie says.

Well it's not like I ain't slept with you, says Bad Fred.

Oh! like you learn all about me by sleeping with me one time. I guess you learn all there is to know about me since you never come back, Connie says.

Oh fuck you, you know why I never come back, jesus.

Connie looks at him, stops drying glasses for a minute and comes over to him. She says, No I don't know why you never come back.

Aw jeez come on, Bad Fred says. You fucking know.

A Chat with the Devil

Then you better tell me what I know, Connie says.

Aw jeez, shit Connie, shit, you're serious ain't you.

Yeah I am, I've been wanting to know, if you want to know.

Aw jeez, the bet with Beverly, you know, jeez, the bet you and Beverly had, come on.

Bet? what bet? Connie says.

Aw fuck, Connie. Big Fred is flustered and he looks at her. Then he wonders, Shit she doesn't know. So he says, Beverly says to me like how she lost the bet you had about how you could get me down on your first time out. I mean I felt like a piece of fucking meat when she said that. You don't remember this?

That bitch. That dirty bitch. Ooooh I'm going to fix her. Listen, I guess you know there was no bet like that. Or hell, maybe there was, maybe I got so coked up that I made the bet, but if I did it was the coke, not me. God I don't know if I should apologize or not.

I didn't know you were into coke, Bad Fred says.

Now and then, Connie says. You know how it is with this crowd, she says, waving her arm at all of the empty stools and tables.

Yeah, I think you should go ahead and apologize. Even if it's the coke, you gotta be sorry for what you do like that.

Connie stacks glasses for a minute. And a lot of feelings happen in her and she almost cries and then she laughs and says, You're right, Fred, I apologize whether I made the bet or not. I mean you're right, I have to be responsible and I'm sorry if I was the cause of you feeling bad like that.

Aw that's okay, I guess I kind of what do you say, fucking overreact I guess.

Connie leans back and smiles at Bad Fred and says, Well.

So. How's things? Bad Fred says.

Could be worse, Connie says. And could be better. I could have a place to live for instance.

How come you ain't got a place to live?

Because my dear old Daddy won't return my phone calls.

Which means fucking what?

Right now I can't afford a place to live and I called Daddy for some money.

So how come he don't return your phone calls?

Oh, he thinks I'll spend the money on coke. I'm asking for three thousand, can you imagine me doing three thousand worth of coke?

One time I sell my Harley and get four thousand and I do coke until all four thousand is gone, Bad Fred says.

Connie doesn't know this about Bad Fred and she looks at him and thinks about how she's not going to fool him. So she says, Anyway, my clothes are all in Vicki's car, and I wait for her to come to work so I can change.

Jeez, what happened to your apartment?

Oh that bastard Phil moves this other chick in and tells me we are all over with and so Vicki helps me move but I don't have any place to move to so here I am, unless I get laid I don't have a place to sleep at night and it's a hell of a way to live, not being able to count on having a bed at night and not having no place to go to after work, Connie says.

Jeez I'd like to help you out, but you know my situation, just one room and the bed alone takes up half of that.

So I have this really great idea, Connie says, and it won't take a hair off your arm, she says. We jack your bed up a foot or so and I live under your bed. You don't lose any space, I gain a place to live. What do you say, Fred, huh? Just until I get the money together for a place of my own?

Bad Fred has this crazy smile on his face. A woman living under my bed? he says.

Connie says, A woman living under Bad Fred's bed. Has a nice ring to it, doesn't it? And maybe I can get on top of the bed sometimes? Could be worse.

Jeez, I guess it's okay, but jesus don't tell anybody about it, Bad Fred says.

A Chat with the Devil

Blue Cream

The way Blue Cream looks, he isn't ready for tonight. The way he looks, he can maybe crash any of several conventions in the city and pass as a Shriner or a dentist or a ventriloquist.

But Blue has just walked into one of the city's more outre night spots (where it's "at" say his sources; meaning "in the swing of it" to Blue). He sticks out like a stunned Baptist conventioneer begging for exit directions at Plato's Retreat.

Almost anyone at all can tell Blue that bifocals and gray hair and a blue oxford cloth shirt stretched over a paunch and a loosened wide blue paisley tie and, yes, his actual bank book in his shirt pocket, create an image not only unlikely to succeed but downright ill-considered.

Life is good, Blue had read, for the mid-life crisis man. Apparently, Blue had read, a man like him is very attractive to younger women. A man like him, however, Blue had not read, is good only while his money lasts, and then only if he tells his firm to find themselves a new vice-president because he is heading for the islands with tools enough to build a boat by hand.

He stands in the second row along the crowded bar, holding two martinis. Now, that's one thing right about him. The other, as it happens, is his name, Blue Cream. He picked it up as a toddler in love with home-made blueberry ice cream and grew to like it so much that he made it his legal name when he turned twenty-one.

Judy Merrifield, after a stout Yankee upbringing and a pale and proper marriage, found herself careening toward 30, panicked, and got out. She discovered on her own that there is no Santa Claus, no tooth fairy. Such discoveries were painful, though, and therefore she avoided discovering that fairy tales were not real. She is still a princess awaiting her magical event, all the while refusing dates and propositions from ordinary men.

Judy can't get to the bar. And Blue is right there.

"Hi! Name's Blue Cream! How about a martini?"

Over the noise Judy comprehends enough to understand he is offering her a new drink called Blue Cream. Though the drink is far from blue or creamy, the glass may as well be an enchanted glass slipper, so spell-binding to her is that unexpected magical name.

Judy thinks the drink is horrid, but the name means everything. Exotic images of castle balls, night air alive with melodies, her prince at hand with the elixir of eternal joy.

Blue is saying to himself, Not bad, not bad for my first try. Blonde, gorgeous, a little shorter than me, looks strong enough to help me build a boat, to balance the mast while I hammer it into the hold.

Blue is feeling the confidence of a man who's never been whipped. He says, "I'm going to the South Seas to build a boat. Would you like to come with me?"

"I don't do sex on a first date," Judy says. She hasn't heard all he said, but there was something about the South Seas and coming together.

And big, bold Blue Cream is embarrassed. Certainly sex is on his mind, but he can't deal with Judy's frankness. It is too noisy to attempt straightening out this conversation with more conversation like this. He's only known Judy for one minute, not long enough to drag her off someplace quiet. Blue becomes giddy, light-headed, chugs the rest of his martini, and decides to say anything at all.

"Fucking-A ditty bag!" Blue says, reaching to his adolescence for this scrotum-scratcher.

Judy laughs and her gesture dumps her martini down the back of her neighbor's jacket where it trickles its way into the carpet.

"I'll get us two more," she shouts. Blue Cream smiles.

Judy pushes her way to the bar and shouts to the bartender, "Two Blue Creams!"

"What's a Blue Cream?" the bartender asks.

Hearing his name, Blue says, "What?"

The bartender says, "With you in a minute, pal."

Judy holds her glass to the bartender's nose. "That's a Blue Cream," she says.

Blue holds out his hand, thinks he's being introduced, announces, "Blue Cream."

The bartender gives him an annoyed look and says to Judy, "That's a martini!"

Blue hands his martini glass to the bartender and says, "Make it two!"

Judy says, "Martini! No wonder it tastes like shit!"

Then to Blue she shouts, "You called this a Blue Cream and it's only a lousy damned martini!"

"My name is Blue Cream! And that's a martini."

"Martinis suck. And so do you." But Judy is hooked.

"Your name is Blue Cream, for real?"

"For real!"

"The South Seas?"

"Build a boat. Sail places."

There are fairy tales like that, aren't there? With boats sailing off into the happy forever sunsets? Judy feels sure there are.

"Can you afford this?" she asks.

Blue pats his shirt pocket and smiles. Also smiling, Judy takes the bank book and raises her eyebrows when she sees the balance. She tucks it back into his pocket, adding pats of her own.

She shouts directly into his ear: "I'll be back in a minute and we can begin our second date!"

A Chat with the Devil

Cambodian Day at the Laundromat

It's Cambodian day at the laundromat and except for a fat lady Jack is the only American in the crowd of little men and women and their little children. Along with the sounds of washers slamming against each other from uneven loads and the clunk and hum of dryers tumbling sneakers and the screeches of children pushing toy cars in the overflowing suds on the floor, there is the chaos of strange language spoken loudly above the din.

While his clothes are washing, Jack has little to do except watch the more attractive of the women, and wonder whether they are twelve or twenty-five years old and wonder what it would be like to make love with a woman so tiny that he could pick her up and slip her on his erection and walk around with her there. One tiny woman carries her baby in a blue canvas harness on her back and Jack thinks that he could wear a harness like that on his front with the woman in it and penetrate her through a hole in the bottom. He could jog that way, he thinks, and each step would make her slide up and down on him.

Jack decides to go sit on the curb out front and smoke a joint while his clothes finish washing. He remembers when he was a boy and automatic washers were invented and Bendix washers had glass doors so people could watch the action, and TV was just getting off the ground and he watched Howdy Doody through a thick curtain of flurrying snow and the reception on the Bendix washer was so clear compared to TV and laundry was so colorful compared to black and white Buffalo Bob and the plot of the laundry action was so open to his imagination compared to the trivial adventures of Clarabelle and Mr. Bluster and stupid Dilly Dally.

When he was ten, the first laundromat opened in his neighborhood and it was right next door and Jack spent a lot of time in there watching the shows on the washers and dryers. The best he remembers is the one about the white snake that was really a terry cloth bathrobe belt.

The snake attacked every other character sooner or later, wrapping itself around them and choking them. There was one episode when the snake gripped a banshee and slammed it over and over into the watery grave in the lower part of the screen only to allow it to escape when it lost interest in the pursuit.

Jack finishes his joint and checks his watch and checks his watch and after a minute he remembers what time the washers should stop and it's about that time so he goes back inside.

Jack is mystified that the tiny people have such huge amounts of laundry, great sacks and baskets of it. All of Jack's laundry fits into one ordinary laundry basket and is in two machines only because the colors and the whites are separated. His machines are stopped so he begins to sort, the permanent press from the rest of it, and sees there is only one dryer free and tries to figure out what to do. Three times he rejects the option of dumping everything into that one dryer, remembering that his shirts will come out wrinkled and make him look like single Dan at the office.

He decides at last to hold the permanent press for the next

available dryer since it is mostly white shirts and makes for tedious viewing, and he dumps everything else into the free dryer which he has been reserving by resting his basket halfway into the opening perhaps for a long time but probably a mere several seconds.

The seats are all taken so Jack picks a place to stand where he can see the reflection of a tiny ass in the glass door of his dryer. The ass belongs to a woman folding a mountain of clothes on the table, a mountain large enough to keep her a major character in Jack's dryer program for some time. The wet clothes are unborn, clumping around, looking dead or not yet alive. But the colors are good and dead or not suggest better things to come. The tiny ass in the glass keeps getting slapped by the wads of clothes, but never reacts. It has apparently survived a great deal in life and finds this less than a minor annoyance.

A Chat with the Devil

The Pickup Lines

Jill looks over the list of men's pick-up lines on the kitchen blackboard, a thing the waitresses do to cheer themselves up.

She hears them. Like five minutes ago she hears number two, Say, what time do you get off, honey? On the blackboard the answer is, Go fuck yourself with a bottle brush, but Jill says, I'm afraid I work way past your bedtime.

Let's get together for a drink later on, it's number five. The answer is, Stick it in a bent pipe. Jill says, You're very kind, perhaps another time.

But as for Farley, the list just says, Watch out for Farley...woman hater.

Jill doesn't know Farley, figures he can't hate women more than she hates men. She gets him tonight, he reserves for eight o'clock. She's in the bathroom crying and tells Joanne, It's no particular reason, just feeling blue, waitress blue.

You must hear this a lot, but you really are a beautiful lady. Number three, answer is, You are so fucking boring. Thank you for saying so, Jill says to the man and that is good for her tip.

A Chat with the Devil

You know, I could really fall for someone like you. Answer is, Just so it's not me, asshole, but Jill says, My compliments on your good taste, and knows her tip is getting bigger than the man's hard-on.

Damn! Farley never gives her a chance to say, Good evening! Jill walks up and he starts talking before she is really there, he's loud enough to cover the distance and it breaks the room into fragments and makes Jill's back feel creepy like everybody is watching her.

Miss, get one thing straight, Farley says, sitting alone at a table on the dark side, and Jill slows down, watches his fiery eyes guide her into place next to his table.

Farley stops a moment like he's interrupted and he stares into Jill's eyes, his face in neutral, his mouth a little open.

Nothing happens and Jill says, Sir?

Jill's father calls her in to punish her and she reports to him, stands stiffly alongside the table in the kitchen; then speaks: Sir? And it is a spanking with his belt on her bare bottom. She snaps her mind back to Farley.

Their bitter eyes don't succeed at putting the other person at warning. It's like she and Farley fire at each other but the shots neutralize. They feel a little naked.

Like a voice from an oil drum, Jill says, May I bring you something from the bar? ending it flat, not like a question.

A glass of bourbon, Farley says through his daze.

On her way back to the bar, a man says, Say honey how would you like to come to work for me? Answer is, How would you like me to jerk out your tongue? Jill walks past with no answer.

She walks around to the back of the bar so she can take some quick looks at Farley. She orders the bourbon like she has only one customer, and Joanne is behind the bar and gives her this little funny look.

You sure you're okay, honey? Joanne says.

Jill looks at her and without moving anything on her face says, Um yeah I'm uh okay, and then glances at Farley like she can't wait another second to make sure he's still there.

Joanne looks over her shoulder and checks out Farley and gives a smile and a shrug to Jill and is busy making drinks.

Her father says, I hate you, you little tramp. And later he says, I need you baby, and he gets weepy. And years go by.

And there is a man who hates like she hates, who hurts like she hurts, and it's Farley and Jill can't strike Farley and realizes that he can't strike her either and in this strange balance she sees they are safe for each other.

She feels wobbly walking the bourbon back to Farley's table, from a nervous kind of relief.

Jill says, I'd be happy to meet you after work tonight. And she thinks, Answer is, I've never had to pay for it in my life, which makes her smile. Farley smiles like he hears it.

Farley says, Yes.

A Chat with the Devil

Tuesday Coke Party

Zeke says, Be sure to come over to my place Tuesday night, man. If things work out, you're gonna see more cocaine than you've ever seen in your life! So I've never done cocaine for lots of reasons like it costs too much and I don't like the idea of feeling problem-free and invincible which is how Zeke described the high to me because you get careless and stupid and I don't like getting careless and stupid.

Smoke doesn't do that to me.

Smoke does mighty fine things to me like enabling me to focus my attention minutely and deeply on anything and detect the underlying reasons why shit happens.

Especially in terms of myself.

I don't mind that at all. I welcome that. Smoke is my friend.

And an occasional tab of acid to give me a little shock therapy when I find myself trapped in some ordinary reality framework and can't see my way out.

That is a friend.

And hash is a friend for giving my lungs fewer puffs of smoke to deal with and for giving me the ritual of the pipe

A Chat with the Devil

which I get off on. These are my friends.

Cocaine does not sound like a friendly drug to me.

But I have decided to try it out and find out for myself.

It's only five-thirty and I'm knocking at Zeke's door already, but what the fuck. Zeke is my friend. No problem hanging out at his place even when that's where I'm waiting to go.

Zeke opens the door, it's too early to ask who is it, and says, Hey, come on in, man!" Walking into Zeke's apartment is a different trip every time.

Once in a while he's home alone, but usually there are people there. Most of the time it's new people, people I never see again. But there are a couple of regulars, Bones and Ralph.

Ralph usually has either his first or his second girlfriend with him, the first being the one who lives with him, and tonight he has the second, a fifteen-year-old slut.

She is white.

I am white.

Zeke and Bones and Ralph are black.

This shit isn't supposed to make any difference, but it does, so what the fuck am I going to do, not point it out? Kiss my ass.

It's a big fucking hypocrisy to think that we can be raised to hate each other and with the passage of a law suddenly erase the whole fucking brainwashing without a trace.

No, it's fucking more difficult than that.

So that's who's at Zeke's when I arrive, Ralph and Trixie and Zeke.

Ralph sits in the recliner and watches TV. Zeke complains to me about him, saying that he don't say shit, what kind of company is that, come over to my house and sit his ass down and watch my fucking TV, man, I don't need that shit, man.

But Zeke is a nice guy, basically, and he don't say this to Ralph.

I don't know what the fuck Trixie is up to. This is the first time I've seen her, and I ask who she is and Zeke says oh this is Trixie.

Trixie says, I ain't never had no sex with a white guy. She says it low so only me and Zeke hear her.

She is a fucking little fox, too. Had her hair all fixed up from a court appearance earlier in the day, real cute face, magnificent ass, and sweet tits for a fifteen-year-old, promising, promising.

I wanted to fuck her right then, man.

But of course I didn't do anything about it because I didn't know who the fuck she was yet and if she was with Ralph well shit, he's twice my size, and she was with him, I soon saw.

A Chat with the Devil

Zeke wanted to fuck her too.

He stood behind her and raised his eyebrows up and down and smiled at me when she did her little rap on me.

I was stoned on hash, but I was cool.

I don't lose my cool when I'm high.

Ricardo once said he liked my style on the street. He said other stoned people look stoned, but I just walk right along like I owned the world, and he imitated me in front of Maxwell's liquor store with all kinds of people around and we both laughed.

We had been kidding around for a few hours at that point and were parting. In his thick Cuban accent, he said I have a good time with you, man.

It touched me.

We had had fun, but I'm used to having fun. Ricardo isn't, apparently.

I sort of expected that Ricardo would be showing up at Zeke's later tonight.

So what the fuck am I supposed to do, faced with a luscious fifteen-year-old who wants to fuck me, one of my dreams come true at last, but there were things wrong with it.

I didn't want to catch instant everything. I didn't want to go to jail that long. So I settled for drooling, which I did all evening.

A Chat with the Devil

I sat on the couch. Lit a cigarette. Trixie was fucking with something in the kitchen. Zeke was pacing around, already nervous about the evening, wondering if it was going to come off okay. Evenings like this happened for Zeke from time to time. He sold cocaine for two dealers, and an occasional cocaine party was inevitable.

Inevitably, Zeke swore off cocaine the next day, the day of the cocaine hangover. For me this was the first time at a coke party. I'd seen snorting various times, that was all. Tonight was freebasing if the coke came through. I had brought along my hash pipe and a gram of hash. There hadn't been any good pot available for over two months, just stale nickel bags, and so I had discovered hash.

I got a really beautiful pipe made out of some kind of stone with brass decoration. Zeke found my paraphernalia amusing and kidded me about it. He laughed when I used the scissors from my Swiss army knife to cut open a packet of LSD tabs.

He laughed at my pinch hitter. I asked him in advance not to laugh when I showed him my new pocket portable smoker, a neat wooden case that holds about a quarter of cleaned pot and a pinch hitter.

Zeke's experience with drugs is from the streets. Mine is from the middle-class. We learn a lot from each other, what it's worth I don't know but it's amusing, both directions.

When the first of the cocaine arrives, an eight-bomber, eight ounces or grams whichever, Zeke goes into action, and I watch with fascination as he takes my cigarette, puffs it up bright and burns a hole in the shoulder of a plastic Coke bottle, and then another on the other side.

A Chat with the Devil

He hands my cigarette back to me after taking a drag and takes a ball-point pen out of the waste basket and scores it twice with a knife, breaks it at the scores and pulls out the refill and sticks the piece of barrel into one of the holes for a mouthpiece.

He almost fills the bottle with water, wraps some foil around the mouth and pricks some holes in it. Presto. In about fifteen seconds I have witnessed the creation of a ghetto bong.

I am fucking amazed.

Here I think we have a work of art to look at for a while, but Zeke just puts it down and rinses out a little creamery bottle that holds an individual serving like for coffee and puts a pinch of baking soda in it and a few drops of water and some cocaine.

He has this frying pan on the stove with the bottom covered with water, and it's sizzling away, and he sits the bottle in the water, to heat up.

He picks it up and swirls it around a little every few minutes, waiting for the coke to precipitate or crystallize or whatever the fuck it's supposed to be doing.

Then it does, and he runs cold water on the outside and he dumps it on a cruddy crumpled up tablecloth to let the liquid drain away.

Then he puts some cigarette ashes in the bowl of the bong and takes a kitchen knife and scrapes the white cocaine goo off the tablecloth and puts it on the ashes.

A Chat with the Devil

There is no courtesy when it comes to Zeke smoking cocaine. He goes first, very simple.

So it gets passed around and I get about six hits during the evening but I never really get off on it, but of course I'm stoned on hash to begin with, I was stoned when I showed up and got stoned a lot more while waiting for the coke to show.

So this Muslim black is there, a really mellow guy once we get high and we stop being black and white so much and we spend the evening looking at each other in amazement as Trixie goes through her various routines.

She is in constant motion, sitting here then hiking there, and she sits next to me for a few minutes then says I'm getting me some white gobble tonight.

Ahmed and I look at each other, fucking freaked.

So we're all crowded into the small kitchen and the more base Trixie becomes the more base we all become.

She is the only chick there except for Susie, Zeke's second girlfriend who stays quiet and off to herself.

And we start telling Trixie she's got a nice ass and would she like to take two of us on at the same time, and she thinks about it and says no, I don't want two men licking me out at the same time.

Me and Ahmed again.

So somebody starts giving her some shit about her tits and she starts rubbing her pussy through her jeans and says well, my tits may not be that great but what I've got down here, this is my little precious.

I get a hard-on, and I figure Zeke's got one too because he's practically drooling on her neck.

Trixie leaves the kitchen and Zeke comes over to me and says in a low voice, what d'ya think, should we get some head off her?

And I say man, I don't want to touch that with nothing, and he tries to talk me into it. He gets me thinking about it seriously but I end up saying nah.

So Bones is there too.

Bones is always where the coke is. He doesn't need an invitation. Nobody really wants him around and since he's around anyway and wants some drugs he gets sent out to deal and deliver so he has a way of fitting in.

Bones has a white stripe up his arm, with a thick glob of skin where his elbow creases, and it's from shooting coke.

Bones is about six-foot-six, lanky, all arms and legs. He cheats people for a living, and living means buying coke because he seldom spends money on anything else.

He cheated me once. I didn't know him yet at the time but I learned about him by giving him $70 for a bag of weed one evening and he never returned.

He was staying at Zeke's place at the time and so I finally filled a garbage bag with his clothes and things so I'd have something to hold against my money. The next morning he showed up and told me that he'd gotten arrested and just got out of jail. It was all bullshit of course and I told him so and

A Chat with the Devil

I told him that he had one day to raise my money and pay me back or I was putting out a $500 contract on his ears and that he had one day to do it.

We talked on the steps for maybe an hour or so and in that time I convinced him that I always spoke honestly, that I never lied and he finally believed my threat.

Bones isn't too bright.

I wasn't sure why I was making a point of honesty that way, but as it turned out it saved my ass. That's how my life goes, there's a lot I never understand at the time but can see clearly retrospect.

He didn't raise shit for money, maybe fifteen dollars and I never saw that, so the following morning I sit on the steps of the building with the bag of Bones's things and a pair of scissors and I cut the living shit out of his clothes and tennis shoes and rackets and leave it all in a pile on the sidewalk.

I wait around for a while, but no Bones so I go inside. Later on, I come out to get cigarettes and the clothes are gone and I step on the sidewalk and there's Bones up the street hollering at me so I sit on the steps and wait for him.

He's all pissed off.

Wha fo you do that to my clothes, man? You crazy, man? Shit man, them's my clothes, man, I git you your money, man, them's my clothes, man, I git you your money, man.

I tell him he doesn't owe me money anymore because that was yesterday.

A Chat with the Devil

So he's flailing his long arms all around hollering at me and getting more pissed and wants to fight me, and I tell the lie that counts because he's going to believe it because he believes I don't lie.

I tell him he won't win.

And he backs off.

Why, because I'm wrong, man? Yeah, man, because you're wrong and I'm right. He bought it and that was the end of the fight.

So Zeke gets me in a corner at one point while waiting for Armand to show up with more coke. There was plenty of it left, of course, but it was time for a break or something.

So Zeke says I gotta tell you about Bones's latest, man. There was like a club of people who had been ripped off by Bones. When Bones ripped you off, you got really pissed because he is so fucking cold about it.

And he does it as if he doesn't care if he's going to get killed over it or not, and there's plenty of people who were out to kill Bones at one time or another, but we always cooled off after a day or two and then Bones knew it was safe to come around again and find somebody new to fuck over.

He never hit the same victim twice, except for Zeke. Zeke was too good-hearted, and he got burned twice so far.

The second time, he was absolutely pissed off, though, and Bones had been staying at his apartment, and he kicked his ass out as soon as he showed up again.

A Chat with the Devil

So there was this club, and we'd hear about others in it from time to time, but mostly we didn't know each other, an exclusive club where the people in it didn't know each other.

So Zeke says Listen to this man, some guy ran into Bones out front and asked him if he knew where he could get some coke, right? And he had three hundred bucks, man, and Bones went for it.

So Bones takes him up the street to the dealer and says he's gonna get three and a half grams for the bucks, man, but the guy comes back a while later and says there's a gram missing. So Bones isn't around, right? And the guy says Bones had damned well better give him a call.

So that should have been the last of Bones for the night, right? But he shows, man, and I tell him he's got to make this phone call that the guy is fucking really pissed off.

So Bones calls the dude, man, and says hey, no problem, I'll just get your money back for you.

So they meet, right, and Bones takes the two and a half grams from the guy and they go to the dealer and Bones never comes out again, and this guy is waiting out front.

So Bones gives the dealer a packet of pure cut, man, he keeps the coke, he gets the three hundred back and he's fucking gone.

So the guy is one pissed off motherfucker, right? I'm laughing my ass off and so is Zeke, because this is probably the best Bones rip-off story so far, a fucking triple burn.

A Chat with the Devil

And Bones keeps on walking, a walking fucking dead man.

And this was like a week ago, and tonight here's Bones again, where the coke is. Everybody waiting for him to get his fucking head blown off, but the months go on and his rips go on and he keeps on walking.

Everybody knows about Bones by now, but there's always a new sucker for him.

So Armand shows up with another eight bomber and there's a pile of coke on the mirror and another pile on the table and people are snorting it while waiting for the stuff to cook. Armand is an arrogant fucking mouth, and he points to the pile on the mirror and says, this is three-cut, man, and I say what's that mean, and he looks at me like I don't know shit and he says man, you don't know shit.

So I say well what's the usual cut when it hits the street, man, and he points to the coke and says this, man, three-cut, fuck man, where the fuck you comin from, man, I ain't talking to you, man, man, and Zeke says hey, this is his first time doing coke, man, and so Armand thinks I'm a fucking cop but I don't give a shit about that, I give a shit about his fucking attitude, so we get to talking about smoke, and Zeke says something stupid about sinse and so I give a little speech about how any kind of weed can be sinse because it only means that the male flowers are picked before they pollinate the females, and even Armand doesn't know this, so he gradually becomes more mellow toward me until at the end of the evening he was being fucking solicitous and I was able to slip in my little put-downs.

Trixie is hot after the coke, and she keeps asking for some and nobody wants to give her any and once when the mirror was kind of empty, she scraped and scraped at it

112

with a razor blade until she got a little snort together, then she licked the mirror, and licked all of the edges of the mirror.

Finally somebody said she could have all the coke she wanted if she would put out.

And she went for it, all the pussy you want for all the coke I want, everybody said yes, Ahmed and I looked at each other and fucking shook our heads again.

So Armand thinks he's cool and Zeke is cooking the coke maybe like the third batch, and he's anxious and saying it's not separating the way it should and he's over the stove bitching about it and Armand says, you don't know how to cook it, man, you ain't cooking it right, man.

Then Armand turns to me and says He don't know how to cook it right, man, he don't know how to cook it.

So he says to Zeke, man, I'll cook the next batch, man, show you how to cook it right, man.

And Armand looks at me again and says, I'll show you how to cook coke, man.

So the next batch comes and Armand tries cooking it by holding the little creamer directly over the flame and like he's burning his fucking fingers, man, because the fucking flame is high, so he doesn't leave it on the flame very long at a time, and it doesn't cook, and he starts bitching and trying to come up with an excuse why it ain't cooking right and he comes up with all this bullshit like there's some kind of dirty shit in the this creamer or something or the flame is too hot or maybe not hot enough, so he fucks it up and finally takes the creamer to the faucet and runs cold water on it and shakes it around and he ends up doing about as good as Zeke did and he passes it off as a good cook.

So the bong is going around, with Zeke in charge of it so it doesn't get too far away from him and so he can get every other hit for himself, and he dips a Q-tip into a bottle of 150 proof rum and lights it to make a torch and lights the bong with this which burns some of Trixie's hair off because the stem on the bong is only like three inches long and her hair sticks out from her forehead in bunches of little curls, and she gets a little pissed but decides fuck it.

Trixie is telling about some fight she got into with her sister, hair-pulling and scratching. It was the baddest fight we ever done, she says, we was fucking wild, fucking out to kill each other. My ma hollers, listen you motherfuckers, quit that goddamned fighting or I'll fucking slam you up against the goddamned walls, you little whore slut pigs, quit it.

And she pulls me off my sister and I be just about to hit her when I see she was gonna hit me, all pulled back, so I said fuck it, ma, I'm done.

And I got my ass out of there.

Trixie was the first time I had ever heard a white girl speaking black English. A white fifteen year old cunt out hoping to score on her first white guy.

What a weird fucking ambition. What after that?

So Ralph starts feeling like it's time to fuck and he wants firsts because Trixie is his chick, he thinks, and everybody thought so at first because she kept calling herself this nigger's woman but as the evening went on she was saying more and more things about general fucking and so Ralph takes her and into the bedroom for a while. Ten Ricardo shows up and does a few hits on the bong and a few snorts off the table and he catches on that Trixie is up for everyone and so he takes her into the living room and pulls her jeans down and tells her to lean over the back of the stuffed chair so he can fuck her from behind, and we're kind of standing around watching because you don't get to see people fucking every day and he's fucking her and decides he wants to fuck her in the ass and starts to put it in there but she starts screaming, don't you fuck my ass you cocksucker, and she tries to reach around to scratch at him and doesn't grab much because he is holding her down, but she does get some digs into his thighs, and Ricardo hollers to Bones, man, hold her fucking arms, will ya, she's fucking scratching my skin off, ow, fuck.

And Bones says hey maybe she don't want to be fucked in the ass, man, and Ricardo backs up a little bit and says, aw shit man, take a look at this, she shits turds twice the size of my pecker, this pecker ain't going to bust her ass, man, hold her fucking arms, man.

So what the fuck, Bones holds her arms and Trixie decides she likes it and starts screaming and Ricardo makes this gesture to Bones, raising up his hand with the palm up, with a grin, saying see, man, she loves it, she fucking loves it.

So the night is getting old and everybody has done all the coke they can stand which never happens and there is coke all over the place, but Zeke wants to deal what's left because he has to pay for some of it, and I go out for some air for a little while and I notice that somebody spilled some coke on the stairs outside the apartment door and Trixie is still licking everything looking for more coke and so finally I tell her that there's a little bit on the steps outside the door and she goes out to snort it up off the step and comes back and says it's not there, just a trace, and Ralph says finally that he sucked it up himself on his way in.

So Zeke sits down and delicately opens what's left in the foil and it's a big rock, man, all that coke left, and he wants it for himself, but he has to sell it to raise the money, so he wraps up some inositol, cut, and sends Bones out to sell it for fifty bucks and Bones goes out and in no time he's back with fifty bucks and he didn't know it was just cut and Zeke says hell that ain't bad, fifty bucks for some cut.

And Bones looks at him and then laughs and says sheeit. So Trixie had to go home at nine-thirty because she promised her social worker that she would be in by ten every night.

And we talk about her, how she is an incredible fucking slut and we wonder about her.

How does a girl get that fucked up that early in life, we say. And how everybody either fucked her or got some head off of her except for me and Ahmed, and how they felt a little dirty about it but it came out like what good head, what a fucking sweet pussy, shit like that, but they were ashamed of themselves for fucking the pathetic little bitch.

And me and Ahmed both say how we really wanted to fuck her but just couldn't make ourselves do it.

It was just empty fucking, and fifteen will get you thirty, and what the fuck did you guys catch tonight that we didn't catch, we're not sucking your dicks, no way, shit like that.

A Chat with the Devil

But I didn't get high off the coke, and Ahmed didn't do any because he brought his bottle of scotch and that's his thing.

I took a few belts off his bottle for old time's sake because I used to be into scotch and he had a jug of J&B which was my favorite.

I keep thinking all night, when are we going to get busted, and at one point Zeke says how this guy he knows was busted on a flight from Miami and had a kilo of coke with him and how his bail was set for a million dollars.

And I'm thinking, nah, this kind of thing goes on all the time, all over town, they don't bust these parties, shit, this is the stratum where things are dispersed among so goddamned many people that it's just pricking pimples to arrest them.

So I relax that way and think well, I'm not going to get arrested.

And Bones decides he wants to see what an LSD tab looks like so I have them wrapped in like foil and stuck in the back of matchbooks and I toss him a matchbook and he gets the tab out and unwraps it and it twiddles its way to the floor, and Bones picks it up and pops it into his mouth.

What I do now, he asks, Shit, what I do wit dis? Susie says swallow it.

And Bones picks it off of his tongue and looks at it and says swallow dis paper? He don't want to swallow no piece of paper, but taking LSD don't bother him at all.

So he swallows it, and this is earlier in the evening and after about an hour and a half it hits and Bones has already shot up with coke at least a few times and he goes paranoid in a complete way I've never seen, or any of us.

And it's scary right off.

Bones pulls his height all the way down to halfway where he is all knees and elbows and he is swirling around in slow motion as if surrounded by tigers, and he swishes around the apartment, and he grabs people and tries to hide behind them and he grabs me, don't grab me, man, fuck, I say and I try to get his hands off me and I can't and I say I almost fought this motherfucker.

And he turns off the lights and he opens the refrigerator door and hides behind it until somebody talks him out of it, and we're all over his case trying to get him to sit down and be still because he's like this huge whirling ball of clubs and tire irons and he's going to bump the apartment into pieces, and he goes into the bathroom and turns off the light and crouches near the toilet, hiding in the dark.

Susie goes looking for him and gets him out of the bathroom.

Then we all try to get him the fuck out of the apartment, let him work this out on the fucking street, man, and not in our faces, and we get him out the door by pretending we're all going for a walk and we put our coats on and get him outside the apartment door and he just turns right around and slinks back into the apartment.

Ahmed tells me his band plays funk and it turns out that it's music that I like but I didn't know there was a name for it like that.

And I'm stoned and I'm thinking that I don't have to belong to my generation or to any generation at all, that I can be all of my life at the same time, and that I don't have to be lower class or middle class but that I can be any class I know how to do all at the same time.

And I'm saying wow because I'm figuring out who the hell I am and how I'd like to be.

But then I start feeling more in control of myself and not just skidding along with whatever the fuck happens to be going on around me, and I look at where I am and how fucking bizarre and scary Bones is, and how we could get busted because everybody is hollering at Bones for a long time and that's noise and how I'd be a first offender, and how I would learn from that, too, just as I have learned a lot tonight, and I go home.

A Chat with the Devil

A Chat with the Devil

Girl-Fishing in Beijing

Our moods finally coincided one night, and suddenly we found ourselves in conversation. I suppose loneliness will eventually nudge anyone over the brink of silence into the higher-risk area of personal interactions.

The further coincidence of finding ourselves in the kitchen all at the same time made the moment feel auspicious for a group experience.

This all-night conversation became thereafter known as TBMF, or The Big Mind Fuck. It was the night we addressed our major issues about living in Communist China, and the night that we shared our paranoia as well as our best girl-fishing stories.

There is an idiom in Chinese that means "I put my hook into the water without bait, so it's your own fault if you get caught." This was my fisherman's technique for catching Dolly, a girl I really wanted, and in fact the technique was given to me by Dolly herself.

I put my hook in the water without bait, and waited for her to bite. Slowly and gently, I reeled her in, unharmed, unthreatened, ready for seduction.

At least, that's how I'll tell it later to my friends. In reality, I myself may have been hooked and reeled in just as carefully and skillfully. I was a high-visibility target in

121

China, a walking, talking moral polluter, and the subject of daily warnings on TV about the American moral pollution threat. How could I know what was actually going on?

This is where paranoia can hold a field day. The usual, comfortable interpretation is that Chinese girls feel trapped in lives on display to inspectors and controllers, and will bite at any hook that promises relief.

There wasn't shit for food that night. We English teachers were on a two-week break, and our cooks took the break, too. The freezers were always stuffed with white bread, mainly because no one ever really wants to eat white bread, and the food of last resort was toast.

"Oh, well," Frank said. "Only two more days and the cooks'll be back." Frank was hovering over the toaster, watching, creating the perfect toast.

Sam said, "I still don't see why the fuck they let the fucking cooks off with five of us still here!" He added, "I know, it's a dead subject now."

We all knew each other, of course. We'd all been together in the dormitory for two months, many longer. We got our food in the kitchen at noon. We shared the computer to get our email. We ran into one or another of us now and then, and we knew each other. On the night of TBMF, it was as if someone had called a meeting, and we were all there.

Sam gave us our daily dose of crude fucking English, and also spared us the bother of complaining about life ourselves.

Skerk! the toaster said, dragging itself to a barely successful pop-up. Frank's toasts were ready.

"You know, our life here isn't really that bad, really," Frank said. And somebody bit, and that got the conversation started. TBMF was now warming up.

"It's nothing I'd want to run away from," Prentice said. "I've got a lot here that I couldn't get at home," he said. "I've got a life here," he stressed, "that I couldn't have at home."

"Yeah, it's not bad," Boomer mused. "God knows it has its good side. If you don't mind being watched."

It was Boomer who got the most paranoid, and he'd get it stirred up in the rest of us sometimes. But this time no one bit.

"What are you complaining about," Prentice said to Boomer. "It seems to me that you have a regular visitor."

"That's just it," Boomer said. "Over here, every one of us has a regular visitor. Or more. Does that mean it's love? Should I marry her? Or am I just another walking passport, another suspect who's being spied on? Shit, man, even you have your regular visitor, and what are the chances of that at your age in Canada?"

"Why ask so many questions?" Prentice shot back. "You're fucking a beautiful young specimen of China's finest. Minimize the bullshit and keep on fucking, that's my advice."

"Is that all that this is about? Fucking?" Sam asked him.

"Isn't it?" Prentice thundered.

Boomer was caught by surprise. The conversation was now beginning in earnest. There had been a double volley.

Suddenly, all five of our minds were asking the same questions. Is fucking really what this is all about? Are we teaching English in Beijing, or are we girl-fishing in one classroom after another? Can we ever really overcome the cultural differences and have a completely intimate relationship? Are we forever doomed to suspecting that our baby doll is really reporting everything to the police? Is it possible to believe anything that a desperate Chinese woman says?

Fucking is what it was all about for everyone, to some degree, because we all got fucked. That was assumed to be a perk of the job after a while.

Chinese girls do not discriminate among men by age. Every age has its good points, and any man of any age will be considered.

Nor do they discriminate themselves by age, granting equal rights to 16- and 60-year-olds alike.

That is, there are no "underage" girls in Beijing. If your hook catches a 16-year-old who is irresistible, you can gently reel her in and you can have her. Her mother will bring her to you on her bicycle after school.

So, girl-fishing is a great sport in Beijing. Even with nothing on your hook, you get a lot of action.

Those thoughts wrapped up Prentice's side of the conversation for the moment.

"Yeah, and I'd like to fucking get something steady, like, well, Teresa's been fucking steady for about seven months now, but she's turning into a bitch. What d'you guys think of her?" Sam asked.

Teresa was tall, slim, pretty. If I'd been taller, I'd have given her a try. But we all let Sam's question slide.

Frank said, "You have to go by their schedules, like if she's a student, give her some daytimes. And if she works, she gets a weekend day, like that. And if you're lucky, you can have a fuck every morning and every evening. That's the way I do it. Of course, you've got to bag a few heads to keep a full schedule."

"Gunny sacks or put a bag over their head?" Prentice asked.

"Over their head!" Frank said. "No, fuck, I'm not going to go scooping them up. Let them come to me. There's always plenty of them waiting."

"Prentice doesn't need a bag for that babe of his," Sam said. "How the fuck can an old man like you attract a babe like that? No wonder this country is fucked up, man!"

"That's what I mean, right there," Boomer piped up. "The only possible explanation is that she's a human sacrifice in service to her country. You all can see that, can't you?" he asked, looking around over his glasses.

He continued, "I mean, I don't care what fucking religion they've got here, or what girls are made to believe about men, some of these combinations simply defy explanation, any other explanation, that is, than a planted spy."

We had agreed to share our best girl-fishing stories. Frank's story had seven girls in it, twice with two of them at a time.

I told my story of Dolly. I had many Chinese girls in love with me, but I waited for Dolly. When I first saw her, I fell in love with her. She was a really special personality, and very beautiful.

Dolly says to me, "In China, we have proverb. Do you hear it? Uhn, do you like hear it, what it say, says? What it's mean?"

I adjust the phone that has been glued to my ear for 45 minutes. "Of course!" I say. "What is it?"

"Ancient Chinese master tell that when go fish, fishing and, you understand?" Yes, I understand. "So when go fish, fishing, only put hook, how you say, not put on hook some thing, you know? Please tell me!" I understand--a hook only, with no bait on it. "Yes, hook only into the water, then, then, if catch a fish it's not your blame. You understand this, this proverb?" I understand it.

I say, "So I put my hook into the water and see what I caught? I caught you!"

"Oh!" she says in a short melodramatic huff. "Oh, I shouldn't tell you this proverb!" She punctuates with sudden pointed whimpers, so delightful that I break out smiling. I listen quietly, hoping to hear a few more.

"Why you say this, this..." she stammers, breaking the silence. "Why you say what, what you caught, you, why you say you caught me! Hmpf!" adding her sharp, short whimper.

"Of course I caught you," I tell her. "I haven't reeled you in yet, that's all."

"Reel me in? Reel? What's reel? How spell?"

"R-e-e-l, pull you in using the string."

"Ah! Ah! Ah! I see. Reel you in. Thank you."

Then the meaning sank in. "You mean, reel me in? No, you must let me free, really!" she says.

"No way!" I say. "I'm going to reel you in smoothly and gently, and then you'll be mine."

"No, don't do," she whimpered. "You must let me free, really. My husband will angry at me, you know?"

"Of course you cannot tell your husband," I say. "It must be our secret, okay?"

I tell the guys how shy she was, how I had to tease her through every step, and how, finally, upon finding herself naked in my bed, she had said, "Shit!" and tossed her head to punctuate a whimper. She stayed in my bed all day.

"So how did you find her?" Sam asked, having followed my story carefully. "Was she the underutilized commodity you expected?"

"In fact, no she wasn't," I said. "She had a well-used pussy; could be she does herself; I mean, she is a gynecologist."

A Chat with the Devil

"But it could also be anything else, too, and that her story is crap, and that she fucks foreigners full-time for the cops and has reported every word you've ever said within her hearing to the police," Boomer pronounced, in one long breath.

"At school, you are the teacher. You always, how you say, same, some... you always just teacher. Now you are not the teacher. You are someone else. I say right?"

Dolly was sitting next to me on the bed, our backs to the wall, the down-filled sheet carelessly draped over her body.

"Who am I now?" I ask.

"I don't know this. You are like lion, like lion," she said. Then shyly she reached for me, held me in her hand and said, "So big!"

She'd been wonderfully responsive to my lovemaking, and seemed to have every erogenous zone in the book memorized. I mean, all of them were turned on and in high gear. That seemed unusual, for usually a woman will have some favorites. Her nipples reddened and hardened quickly and were sensitive enough to bring a climax. She didn't seem to be faking.

Prentice said, "But how would we ever know for sure that we're not all being catered to by trained operatives!" Prentice was now voicing Boomer's concerns. "I mean, here's this woman whose husband very seldom sleeps with her, who hasn't been pregnant, who says she has no other sex life, yet her pussy is half worn-out at age 24. What's wrong with this picture?"

A Chat with the Devil

Actually, none of us wanted to see what was wrong with our pictures. This was the good life. Good food, good housing, easy job, good money, and all the girls we could catch from the stream. No bait needed.

A Chat with the Devil

The Rustle of Taffeta

The city doesn't have a name. The sidewalks are a bluish felt and the streets are dull black. The waist-high pipe railings are candy-cane red and always look freshly painted. The slim, blonde girls are all eighteen and they all wear short taffeta skirts that rustle with invitation.

It seems that I am the only man in this city. I know that I can bend any girl over the railing at any time. I know they expect it. I don't know if they hope for it, but I do know that they never protest. I wonder if I have ever bent a girl over the railing before, and I wonder why I'm not very interested in doing it now.

The air is fresh, perfect for a walk. I seem to float along. The traffic is silent and the only sound is the sound of air, a quiet white noise. I'm not going anywhere. I'm just walking, or floating, along. Time isn't pressuring me to do anything or to arrive anywhere. My mind isn't active; it seems to be in a state of prolonged stun, a thickness, a white fudge.

I suppose that I am walking for pleasure, or because I began walking with some purpose that has now vanished and I continued walking. The street seems endless and all the same. The cars only seem to be moving because I see the same cars in the same places whenever I look.

A Chat with the Devil

On the sidewalk, the girls pass on both sides of me, all going in the other direction. None of them looks at me. I notice that they all have polka-dot skirts, white polka dots on black taffeta. From this, I know that they all wear white panties, and that their cheeks are perfectly round. I twist to my left to look behind me, to look at the backsides of the girls. A wind blows their skirts up and I see their white panties.

I look at my own clothing and see that I'm wearing a sky-blue sports coat and white pants and a white shirt and brown shoes. This outfit seems unusual to me, but these colors make me feel light and carefree. I begin to wonder if I really am myself, but then I think about the sky-blue color of my coat and I wonder if my eyes are blue.

I look at the eyes of the girls passing by and notice that all of them have blue eyes. The girls each look different, yet everything about them seems the same. They all have curls hanging down in front of their ears, blonde curls that were made by spooling the hair on pencils and then coating it with syrup.

I wonder if they would all feel the same if I bent them over the railing. I wonder if I lined them all up and tried each one in turn if there would be any difference among them. I wonder if my white pants would fall down or if I could tie a string to the back of the waist and loop it over my shoulder to hold them halfway up.

The girls are wearing black broad-brimmed hats. They are wearing black pumps that barely contact the felt sidewalk. I notice that they are carrying take-out bags of coffee and donuts. I suppose they are all going to their offices. I imagine that they get bent over their desks and that their hats fall on the floor.

A Chat with the Devil

I go into an office, up the stairs that pass the library and the editor's office. I see the girls bent over the desks and the men behind them reading manuscripts. I look closely at the desk nearest me and see that the girl is eating a donut, and that her hat is on the floor. The man behind her has his pants held up by a string attached to the waist, and the string is looped around his shoulder.

I hear the sound of taffeta rustling throughout the room. I wonder if anyone is drinking the coffee. I look around to see if there is a cup of coffee that no one seems to want, that I could take for myself. I see a cup on a nearby desk. The blonde girl doesn't look at me as I reach for it; she just takes another bite of her donut. I feel this is her way of giving me permission to take the coffee.

I look around to see if there is any girl who is not bent over her desk, but they are all occupied. I go down the stairs and float along the sidewalk. All of the girls are gone now, gone to their offices, I suppose. I am alone on the sidewalk. I have an itch in my groin. I look around and see no one, so I reach down and scratch it. I try to remember what color my shorts are, but cannot. I try to remember if I drank the coffee, but cannot.

There is no traffic on the street now. The sun is bright but there are no shadows. I roll up my shirtsleeves and wonder what happened to my sports coat. I suppose I must have spilled the coffee on it and left it in the office. I wonder if I have a job somewhere, an office that I should be in now, a girl to bend over my desk while I read manuscripts and listen to the rustle of taffeta.

A Chat with the Devil

www.ingramcontent.com/pod-product-compliance
Lightning Source LLC
Chambersburg PA
CBHW020702030726
47498CB00002B/599